The Last Sketch

Gosia Nealon

INDIES UNITED PUBLISHING HOUSE, LLC

INDIES UNITED PUBLISHING HOUSE, LLC
P.O. BOX 3071
QUINCY, IL 62305-3071

*To the lost generation of young people
whose dreams faded away with the war.*

Part I

"When I hear him play Beethoven's 'Moonlight Sonata,' something good dies in me. I stare at my blood-stained hands and then at the devil who's playing Tata's piano. And as the cuckoo clock announces another hour, I vow to myself that one day, I will kill the monster."
~Wanda Odwaga

1

Wanda

I move along with crowds of people and a swirl of pigeons. One word trumpets over and over: *Łapanka*. Roundup. Unable to think straight, I rush down a cobbled street toward the ruins of Royal Castle. Overhead, the giant clouds curse me with continuous drizzling rain, but I'm more determined than ever to escape all this madness.

Jostled by people with unfamiliar faces, I just want to reach Castle Square and disappear into one of its alleys, but the German tarpaulin-covered lorries are already upon us. Halted by a swarm of armed soldiers, women cry, and men curse. The body of a man killed mid-run lies on the pavement in a puddle of blood. I can't help but think how easily life can be taken away in a few seconds. Maybe right now someone is waiting, worried sick about him, the same way I have been worrying about my brother.

I step backward and shrink behind a tall, older man in a felt hat and raven overcoat. When I'm able to steady my breathing, I clutch to my chest a small package wrapped in brown paper—*Biuletyn Informacyjny*, a forbidden journal with anti-Nazi propaganda. The last thing I need is to be classified as a political prisoner, and I will be if they find it on me. I have to dump it into that pile of rubbish behind me. But I don't want to, so I helplessly search for a cellar window I could escape through. It's how Mateusz once fled from another roundup.

Then I feel a gentle pull on the back of my coat. A one-armed boy waves me into a tiny passageway. Since I'm behind the crowd, the German soldier across the way most likely can't see me. I know it's my only chance of a getaway, so I watch the soldier with a wild heartbeat. The moment he looks away from the crowd, I swallow hard and squat backward, expecting to be shot at any moment.

After squeezing through the tiny passage, I settle next to the little boy who now lingers behind the pile of rubbish. Still trembling, I wipe the sweat from my forehead.

A smell of a dead animal makes me almost choke, but at the moment, I'm more concerned about the cement wall in the rear. The only way out of this small alley is via the main street. I can't help sighing in despair.

The boy gestures for silence by pressing a finger to his lips.

I nod without another peep. This child is smart for one so young. Why is he here alone and not at home with his parents? Are they caught in the roundup too? Maybe they just couldn't hide with him since there's so little space here. For the first time, I thank the Creator for making me petite.

A moment later, it all begins—a clang of rifles fired into the air and desperate cries from people. Soldiers bark, "*Schnell!*" to keep everyone from crowding.

As the trucks drive away and the commotion dies down, I struggle to move, paralyzed by the thought of what would happen to the captured people. I press my palm to my chest and try to suppress sorrow. It's my first roundup, but lately, they have been more frequent and done in retaliation for the resistance activities. The thought of the Germans punishing random people turns my stomach. They basically drive through Warsaw and take anyone who happens to be in the wrong place at the wrong time. Hitler wants to terrorize us into submitting. But I know very well that will never happen. We won't stop until this damned war ends and we get our freedom back.

We stay in the hideout until the street is peaceful. The boy's blue eyes squint at me from his gaunt, dirty face. He's wearing a muddy overcoat that dwarfs him. Someone does care for him, though, because his coat is full of patches. He looks to be no more than five or six.

An uncomfortable lump builds in my throat. "What's your name?" I ask.

"Kubuś," he says, his lips are chapped and his gaze is fixed on the ground.

I smile to encourage him. "Do you live somewhere around here?"

He looks at me with horror. "Grandma didn't wake up." His hand trembles as he wipes his tears.

"Where are your parents?" I must bring him home to his worried family.

He stares at me. "Only Grandma."

"Let me take you back to your grandma, Kubuś. I'm sure she is waiting. Can you show me where you live?"

He shakes his head and adds, "She went to heaven."

It pains me to hear it but I'm not sure if he is telling the truth. I long to cheer him up a little bit, so I say, "Thank you for being so brave and for helping me."

Despite tears, a shy smile quivers at his mouth. "I saw you behind all the other people, and you looked so scared," he says. "And the bad soldiers were still far enough away for you to hide."

There is no way he can survive much longer without help, not if he tells the truth about his family. I can't just walk away.

"Listen to me, Kubuś." I kneel and touch his only arm. "I need you to trust me. I have to take you back to your home, and if there's no one there, we will grab your belongings and go to a place with good food and clean clothes." I hug him. "I promise."

* * *

With slow, cautious movements, we head north. I take comfort in the fact that Świętojańska Street is empty. It's good to inhale clean air again. Out of habit, I stop next to a wooden kiosk covered with announcements and smile at Kubuś with assurance. "I have to take a quick look at something, and then we can go."

He nods and tightens his hold on my hand.

I look for red German posters with names of Poles held in the Pawiak Prison and sentenced for execution in the ghetto ruins or other unknown places.

After finding a new notice with a long list of names of people to be executed in two days, I close my eyes and gather all my strength to read through it. I wipe sweat from my forehead and scan the list, hoping my brother's name is not on it.

When I'm done, I exhale with relief. One more announcement confirms a chance Mateusz is still alive, although I suspect they haven't been posting all their victims' names. They would not have enough paper to do so. I survey the list once more and then whisper a prayer for the condemned people.

Once more, I convince myself that my funny, ridiculous brother is still alive. I would give everything to hear one of his silly jokes again.

"Let's go, Kubuś," I say, but as I turn around, I bump into someone. To my horror, the package lands under the feet of a stranger in a faded khaki jacket. We kneel at the same time, but the man puts his hand on it first. I'm astonished by a mixture of arrogance and strength combined with a trace of softness in his smoky eyes. My belly flutters.

When we stand up, he hands me the package, a smile flickering across his face. Something is intriguing about him, but I can't grasp what. Maybe the woodsy scent that brushes my senses, or the way he combs his dark blond hair back for a smooth look.

"Thank you," I say, hating the shaky sound of my voice. For a brief moment, I wish I had put more effort into looking decent. I'm far from stylish in my tattered overcoat, a simple braid twisted at the crown of my head. But why would I care what this stranger thinks of me? These days, it's necessary to melt into crowds.

"*Prosie.*" He speaks with accented Polish.

Did he just call me a piglet? No, I'm sure he meant to say *proszę*, you're welcome. I can't suppress my laugh.

He extends his hand toward me and says, "I'm Finn."

When I take it, he kisses my knuckles. I try not to blush, and I want to scold my heart for skipping in such a chaotic way. This man looks at me as if I'm beautiful and interesting. I like it.

"I'm Irena," I lie. It doesn't matter how charming he is; I still can't risk giving away my true identity to strangers.

Before he can say anything else, I take Kubuś's hand and scamper away.

When we turn onto Miodowa Street, the man is still standing in the same spot, watching us, which gives me an uneasy feeling. Is he a spy? He has such intelligent eyes, yet mysterious at the same time. And those faded clothes he wears —a camouflage?

I chase away my thoughts of him and concentrate on finding Krucza Street and the red-brick tenement where Kubuś tells me he lives. After a brisk walk, we enter an iron gateway and walk through an empty courtyard. No one stops us from entering the building, so we climb the staircase to the second floor and knock at the door with the number five in its center. I can sense the little boy's distress as he hides behind me. That's not a good sign.

It takes me several minutes of knocking before the door swings open and a skinny, young woman with a tired but friendly face appears. The smell of boiled potatoes and cabbage swaddles me.

"How can I help you?" she asks as a baby's cry emerges from inside. Then two little boys appear and pull at her apron while wailing for food.

I know there is no point wasting time explaining, so I pull Kubuś out from behind me. "I found this little boy wandering the streets. Is he yours?"

She glances at him and shakes her head. "We only moved in yesterday, but I know the prior tenant died of a heart attack, and a little boy went missing a couple of days ago." She ignores all the commotion behind her and continues in a quiet voice. "Maybe that's the boy. I already have four mouths to feed, so I can't take him." She sighs. "I'm so sorry. I wish I could help."

I somehow know this woman is telling the truth, and there

is no trace of hostility in her. "Do you know if he has any other family?"

"I truly don't know. But you should ask the watchman. The first door on the left when you enter the building." She comes closer to me and whispers, "Be careful though, as he's a Volksdeutscher."

I nod. "Thank you for your help." It's clear she doesn't know anything else, so I follow her advice and go looking for the watchman. We find him sweeping a courtyard.

He recognizes the little boy right away. Pointing his broom at him, he says, "Where were you, charlatan?" He flashes a toothless smile.

Kubuś doesn't smile back or answer. Instead, he grips my hand tighter, and I know that the man can't be trusted, or at least the boy doesn't like him for some reason.

"He was lost in the streets," I say.

The man takes his hat off and wipes sweat from his wrinkled forehead. "And who are you?"

I decide to ignore his question. "I'm looking for the boy's relatives, sir. Do you know where I can find them?"

He tosses the broom away and folds his hands at his chest. "You can just leave him with me. This child has no one else and he owes me money anyway, so he can work it off."

Is this a joke? Did he just say that the little boy owes him money? I want to laugh in his face just to show him how ridiculous this is. There is no way I will leave the innocent child with this skunk.

"I work for the Department of Social Welfare, and I was sent to check this boy's living situation," I lie, hoping he won't ask me for proof of identification.

He arches his brow, and his relaxed demeanor vanishes. "He only had a grandmother who was renting the flat on the second floor, but she passed away a couple of weeks ago. The boy doesn't have anyone else, so I took him to live with me, but he ran away two days ago."

"And you're sure he doesn't have any other relatives?"

"His mother died in labor, and he was born with only one arm. No one knows who his father is." He spits on the ground, and a trace of disgust crosses his face. "He's useless to me, so I was going to take him to the orphanage."

"I'll take care of that. Where are his belongings?" It takes a lot of inner resolve to not explode at this man.

"There is nothing left. His grandmother owed four months back rent, and the furniture wasn't hers anyway. The rest I sold to get at least some of the money back." He gives me the kind of look he thinks should make me feel sorry for him.

I know arguing won't get me anywhere and I need to take Kubuś as far from this place as possible. "What about family pictures or documents?"

"They came and took it as it was."

How I want to smack this man and shake him until he begs me for mercy. Instead, I thank him and walk away before he starts asking questions.

When we are outside the iron gate, I kneel and look at Kubuś. "Don't worry. I'll take care of you."

"Thank you for not leaving me here. He likes to yell at me and makes me sit on the sidewalk and beg for money."

That man is a piece of work. I feel anger in every fiber of my body, but I manage to say through my clenched teeth, "You don't have to worry about him anymore. Now let's go have something good to eat." At least I'm able to offer him that much. I expect Mama will throw a fit, but I can always count on Tata's support.

It's too late to deliver the package to Witek, who by now has gone on a mission outside of Warsaw. He warned me not to be late and not to leave it with anyone else. So I have to bring it back home, and that triggers more risk. Taking a trolley is out of the picture due to frequent searches.

I sigh. "We have a long walk ahead of us."

* * *

"How good to see you, my friend," I say a moment later to Jacek, who stands on the sidewalk with his rickshaw." I fight the urge to ask him for help, as I'm already risking the little boy's life by letting him accompany me while I'm carrying the journals. "No clients, huh?"

"Hello, Miss Wanda." A shy smile lights his freckled face surrounded by spiked red hair. "I'm done for the day." He glances at Kubuś. "Can I be of any help?"

"We are heading home."

"That's a long walk," he says, not taking his gaze off my package. "Let me give you a ride."

I hate to put him in danger, but I really dread the long walk, so we climb into his rickshaw while a wave of guilt consumes me.

He points at the woolen blanket covering the seat and says, "I'm glad I brought it with me today." He pulls the bike off the sidewalk. "You may use it to cover the package."

I expect no less from this sixteen-year-old, who risks his life every day carrying messages for the resistance. Still, it pains me to think he could get into trouble for helping me. I put the package under my feet and cover our legs with the blanket. It would be easier if I threw the journals away, but something stops me from doing it. I know how much work it takes to create them. I know how important they are for people like me. They remind me that this stupid war has to end one day and that my life will go back to normal; that Poland will be Poland again.

The ride to Żoliborz—the northwestern district of Warsaw on the left bank of Vistula's river—turns out to be peaceful. There are only a few passersby on Śmiała Street, and they pay us no attention.

My Żoliborz smiles at me, with the early signs of spring captured on white trees. I like it that way the most as it reminds me of my childhood years. Next month, it will bloom into its full verdant beauty, with white houses and villas surrounded by extensive parklands.

My daydreaming ends when Jacek slows down.

"*Szkopy.*" Germans. That one word he whispers makes my skin shiver. Will this day ever end? It's one thing after another, and there is no time to even think straight.

Kubuś lets out an almost inaudible whimper, so I put my arm around him. "We'll be fine," I say with forced assurance. "Just stay still."

But my mind is far from calm. I push the blanket down to my feet to make sure the package is fully buried in it. I swallow hard. More than anything, I want to cry. Yes, I want to cry just like I did when I was little, and I didn't know what else to do when Mama was upset with me.

Two soldiers in steel helmets and gray overcoats block the road with their three-wheeled motorbike, submachine guns pointed at us.

"*Halt.*" One of them walks forward, glaring at me. "*Kennkarte.*" ID card.

I dig out my forged papers that show my name as Irena Malecka and my employment in the German sewing factory, *Helga*, in the city center. It's easier to get away with things if one works for the Germans.

He studies my papers with a rather unintelligent expression, or that's how it seems. He is young, though, so I wonder if I should put on a smile and flirt with him, acting polite and sweet. That sort of behavior had saved my skin quite a few times when, in the end, soldiers just tipped their hats at me and waved me through. Hopefully it works that way this time too.

He raises his head, and his pale blue eyes glower at me. "Get down."

A film of cold sweat covers my body. If we get off, he will notice the package and ask to open it. Maybe he won't search the rickshaw, but we have to climb off without uncovering the damn package.

"Sure, Officer," I say, to steal some more time and bat my eyelashes at him. "It's so nice to see such handsome men keeping the streets of Warsaw safe." I smile and look at him with admiration, like I would look at any dashing young man.

At first he seems baffled by my behavior, but soon enough the harsh expression on his face softens, and he smiles at me while checking me out.

"How's your day so far, Officer?"

He relaxes his grip on the submachine gun and leans in closer. "I can't complain, since my shift is almost over." His gaze lingers on my lips. "How about your day, pretty girl?"

"It's been boring, at least until now," I say, batting my lashes again.

He chuckles. "Well, I'm looking forward to good food and nice music at Café Greta. Would you like to join me?"

I don't like the smug look on his face, but if I refuse, he won't take it in a dignified way.

I pretend to be thrilled with his invitation. "Sure, what time will you be there, handsome?" He can wait a whole night but he won't see me there, that's for sure.

"We are about to head there now, sweetie, and I have a room for you too." He grins. "Have the rickshaw boy drive this little boy home. I would hate if something happened to him."

No, absolutely no. It's not how this is supposed to go.

Maybe I overdid the flirting. This is the first time I've actually been invited on a date by a soldier. A tiny tremor runs all over my skin. I have to get out of this. He's supposed to just smile and let us pass.

As the adrenalin surges through my veins, I know my only hope is to fabricate a story, so he'll change his mind about spending time with me tonight.

"That sounds amazing, and I can't wait to join you. And thank you for letting my brother get home safe. He's been through a lot, as he is infected with typhus," I say and sigh. "He is such a poorly child." I take out the right sleeve of Kubuś's coat and wave it in the air. "Last time, they had to cut off his arm."

As Kubuś makes soft, screechy sounds, the soldier straightens, twists his face in disgust, and throws my papers at me. "Get out of here, bitch." He turns and walks away without another glance.

I'm too dazed to fix the blanket at our feet, so I just quickly signal Jacek to move on. When he has pedaled far away from them, he says, "That was a close one."

I nod and try to get rid of the shaky feeling. Tata told me once that Germans are terrified of any infectious diseases. That piece of information has saved our lives. At the age of twenty-three and in the fifth year of this murderous occupation, every day I hope I will return to my family. It's like I have been waiting for the inevitable to happen, and I don't know when. But not today. Not yet.

2

Wanda

THE SIGHT of our white cottage, hidden in the shade of an enormous silver spruce, is a balm to my anxious mind.

"Why don't you stop by?" I say to Jacek, who gets down to open the iron gate.

"Next time, Miss Wanda. I have to get back before curfew."

I can't restrain myself from kissing this daring boy on the cheek, which ruffles his usually calm demeanor. I pretend not to notice. "Come over soon."

He nods. His cheeks turn pink when he hands me the package. "Good night."

As he closes the gate behind us, we walk through the garden to the side door. The series of piping calls—*chuck-chuck-chuck*—make Kubuś raise his head and glance at the woodpecker working hard on the silver spruce.

"At least he's not drilling on our roof this time," I say, and I can't help but smile.

The sweet scents of apple and cherry trees mingle in my nose and travel through my other senses. It feels so good to be home.

The house appears silent until the clanging sound of pots and pans emanates from the kitchen. Mama must be in one of her moods. I open the adjoining double door. Tata sits at our dining table, small glasses fixed on his nose, screwing something on his radio set. Our elegant crystal chandelier hangs above him like his guardian angel, complemented by the Persian wall rug showing two peacocks perched on a tree, vestiges of our better times.

Tata is a rule-breaker, especially when it comes to any decrees imposed by the Nazis.

"Hello, Tata. You know Mama doesn't like it when you take out your radio set." I can't stifle a laugh. "Please, at least no Chopin today, or she'll have a heart attack." Both activities are punishable by death.

Despite the salt-and-pepper hair and wrinkled face that show his seventy-one years, my father is still full of life.

"There you are, sunshine." When he looks at me, I see a wave of relief passing across his tired face. "Yes, yes—no fellow Chopin today, indeed."

Although he retired from his medical practice six years ago, he still volunteers at a hospital. After our savings vanished from our bank account, he found a way to support us so I can continue my English studies in the underground university. The weekly ticket rations allowed are not enough to survive, so Tata distills moonshine in the basement. He sells it and buys food on the black market with the profits. All of this is illegal, but if we were to stick only to the food rations, we would starve.

When Tata's gaze shifts to Kubuś standing next to me, surprise appears on his face.

"And who is that handsome little fellow?" he asks, a puzzled but welcoming look in his eyes.

Mama stands at the kitchen door with her hands folded

across her chest and her face wearing a solemn expression.

"I will tell you everything, but let's feed this little boy first," I say, feeling a sudden lack of energy. My mother knows how to exhaust me.

"Oh, yes, yes—he is probably starving." Tata ushers us into the kitchen.

* * *

After dinner, I bathe Kubuś and dress him in an oversized but clean cotton shirt I found in my brother's old bedroom. I decide he should sleep in there.

I tuck him under the covers, still able to trace a warm hint of Mateusz's cologne, even though he hasn't slept here in ages.

"Would you like a bedtime story?" I ask, restraining myself from yawning. Perhaps after a good night's sleep, things will look brighter.

He nods. "Does he have a name?" His focus is on an old teddy bear in his embrace.

"You can name him however you like, sweetheart. When my brother was little, he called him Misiu."

His face lights up. "I like it. Do you know why he has only one eye?"

"I'm not sure," I say. "But I can assure you this bear is special since he is still here. My brother used to like to perform surgery on his toys." I laugh. "And now he is a doctor."

"Grandma said I'm special too because God needs my arm in heaven," he says, his voice breaking. "But sometimes I wish he'd give it back to me."

I feel tightness in my throat. I have no experience talking to little kids, so I'm afraid I will somehow hurt his feelings, whatever I say.

I make steady eye contact with him. "Your grandma was right—you are unique, and you proved it today."

"I miss her. Do you know why she didn't wake up?"

I try to choose my next words with care. "I know it's difficult to understand it, but sometimes people just don't wake up. For sure, your grandma is looking over you from above." I look up. "She is your guardian."

His face is even sadder now. I guess my answer doesn't help soothe his pain. Perhaps I should ask Tata to talk to him about it.

"Grandma said Mommy is my guardian angel. She is in heaven too."

Poor child. According to what the watchman said, he has no one. "Do you know where your daddy is?"

"I only have Mommy," he says. "I have her photo in my coat. I'll show it to you tomorrow."

"I can't wait to see it." I have to help him as much I can.

He yawns. "You promised me a story."

"Of course, sunshine. Do you know the one about the seven dwarfs?"

"No."

Before I finish it, he is already asleep.

I long to bathe and climb into bed, but my parents are expecting me. Tata would be fine if I didn't come, but Mama would have a fit. I bet right now she is deciding on the most effective lice cure. I sigh and go to the kitchen. Tata sits at our small table drinking ersatz coffee that Mama made from acorns. We have learned to appreciate it in the absence of real coffee, now that we're used to its bitter walnut taste.

Feeding Kubuś turned out to be an effortless task. He gulped Mama's caraway soup, which had a spicy aroma but a sweet and sharp flavor. He also chowed down a piece of black bread with delight on his face, even though we all hate it for its bitter taste and unchewable texture.

Now, Mama is still bustling near the white-tiled wood-burning stove with sets of black pots and wooden spoons hanging on the wall above it.

"I have this old cure for lice," she says, taking off her apron and joining us at the table. As she runs her skeletal hand over the tablecloth, her hazelnut eyes settle directly on me.

"I found none on him. I don't think he was out on the streets for very long."

"Is he asleep now?"

"Yes." I pause, trying to choose the right words. "He is such a sweet boy, Mama. He likes Mateusz's old teddy bear."

For a moment, she remains silent, though a flicker of irritation shines in her eyes. Since my brother vanished a year ago, my mother has become a living ghost. Her tall figure is even bonier now, and the inky hair gathered in a knot at the back of her head looks dull. In her mid-fifties, she is still beautiful, but there is no life in her anymore. If she's not cooking, she sits in Mateusz's old room, looking at his things as if they were sacred.

"Misiu," she whispers. "That's what he called his teddy bear when he was little."

I want to hug her and tell her it will all turn out fine, but there is a wall between us that we have both been building for years. Mama always adored Mateusz, who grew to have shiny black hair, a handsome face, and a tall figure like hers. I think Tata saw it too and tried to make it up to me.

"You are my beautiful princess," Tata said to me so many times. "Don't ever forget this, sweetheart."

The best memories from my childhood revolve around spending time with him. He taught me how to play piano and to love Chopin; he taught me how to see other people's struggles and not walk away; he taught me how important it was to believe in myself. He was the one who consoled me over my first heartbreaks, and he was the one I always came to when I needed a hug or a shoulder to cry on.

"You have a rare talent," he said to me another time. "But if your heart tells you to take another path, listen to it."

I had the kind of relationship with Tata that most of my girlfriends shared with their mothers. Mama was an enigma to me. As a teenage girl, I viewed her as a beautiful swan, while I was an ugly duckling with my dull, dark-blond hair.

I tell my parents how I found Kubuś and what happened to me. "As you see, he saved me," I say. "I have to help him as much I can."

"You need to find out his address and take him back there. I'm sure someone is waiting for him," Mama says, a determined look on her face.

"I went there, and the watchman of the building said he has no one. It's easier if he stays here for now."

She glares at me. "You don't know if he told you the truth."

"Calm down, honey." Tata's voice is soft but powerful. "This little boy will stay with us until we find out more about his family."

"Honey—" Mama is interrupted by a soft knock on the door.

I scramble to the window and gasp at two black cars and soldiers. My heart freezes.

"Gestapo," I say, unable to control the panic in my voice. I glance at Tata, who has already dashed into the family room. How come we didn't hear car engines outside?

We follow him.

"Where is your package?" he asks without looking at me, his voice eerily calm.

"In the hideout under the floor."

When another knock comes, Tata glances once more at us and shuffles toward the door.

I want to yell at him not to open it, but we all know we have no choice. In the end, they will get in here regardless of what we decide to do. But that calm knock on the door seems out of place, as if there are no soldiers just outside our window.

Mama and I hover behind Tata as he prepares to open the door. But the second he does, a cold numbness washes over me. It is the same stranger I bumped into earlier in the Old Town, but this time he wears a gray uniform with the letters SD. His eyes seem different now—cold and empty. Is he here to see me? Or is this just a coincidence since there are soldiers outside?

"Hello, Doctor Odwaga," he says in a polite voice. "I'm SS-Hauptsturmführer Stefan Keller and I'm here to speak to you on an urgent matter."

He lied before when he said his name was Finn. I swallow hard and step backward, afraid he'll remember me, but when he glances at me, there is no hint of recognition in his eyes, as if he is seeing me for the first time.

"How can we help you, Officer?" Tata's voice is calm.

A cynical smile twists the stranger's lips. "Do you mind if I come in?" he asks without taking his eyes off Tata's face.

Tata waves him in, and they both sit at our dining table. So far he's given no indication of recognition, so I know he did not come here for me. But why is he here? And why did he leave the other soldiers outside? I have a feeling this man is a manipulative bastard and he is going to play games to get whatever he is after.

Once Mama serves coffee, she takes my arm in a gesture to leave the room, but the man says, "Please ladies, join us."

His deep voice seems to vibrate along my nerves, but I obey and follow Mama to take a seat on Tata's side of the table.

The man focuses on Tata. "I have heard many compliments

about your practice, Doctor." He takes a sip of the ersatz coffee and there is a sign of distaste on his face.

"Thank you, Officer. I'm retired now but I truly enjoyed my profession through all these years."

"War doesn't allow people to retire." He gives a brief laugh. "Furthermore, we are in need of skilled people like you."

"It would be an honor to serve you with my knowledge and skills, but if only I were ten years younger," Tata says, sighing. He takes his hand out. "This terrible arthritis in my hands doesn't allow me to operate anymore, and my sight is not the sharpest these days." What a wonderful liar my father is.

The man nods without taking his cold, composed eyes off Tata's face. "I see. Though, I think you misunderstood me, Doctor. I do respect you, but I have someone else in mind."

Is he talking about Mateusz? An uncomfortable silence hangs between them as they stare at each other. It feels as if we have a ticking bomb in the middle of our family room. As if our destiny is in this stranger's hands, who at any time could call on the soldiers outside and order our destruction.

Tata clears his throat. "I have been out of practice for years, so I have no other doctors to recommend at this time," he says in a rather weak voice.

"Your son has been known for his brilliant and innovative approaches, correct?" His voice is so quiet and tense that I find myself forgetting to breathe for a moment.

My father's laughter rings out and he makes a dismissing wave with his hand, as if what the man just asked for is not worthy of consideration. "In my opinion the only brilliant doctors and lawyers are being produced by the Third Reich."

The man doesn't laugh back or even smile. "Do you know where I can find him?"

When Tata doesn't answer, he shifts his now darkened eyes to me. A cold tremor runs through my body. I try not to show it.

An evil look flashes across his face. "You have a delightful daughter, Doctor. My men,"—he gestures to the window—"very much enjoy young and fresh girls like her."

A sudden wave of bulging anger rises to my throat, and I have this overwhelming need to smack him. Instead, I lean forward, snap a porcelain cup in front of him and splash coffee on his despised uniform." At first I enjoy the initial sign of shock in his eyes, but only until the cold realization of my terrible act clenches at my core. I can't believe I've just done something so stupid. I'm an idiot.

Mama gasps and springs toward the kitchen, and a second later she comes back with a towel. While she busies herself cleaning his uniform, the man sits straight-backed, with his gray eyes blazing into mine. The hatred emanating from him makes me tremble. He is going to kill me. He is going to kill us all because of my impetuous and senseless act.

"Please forgive my daughter, Officer." My father's voice sounds so desperate that my heart cries. "She is so young and impulsive."

"Shut up, you fool!" The German bangs his fist on the table, and we freeze.

The eerie silence is broken by gentle footsteps coming our way, followed by Kubuś's voice. "Miss Wanda, I'm thirsty."

The man gives a harsh laugh, and seconds later the door swings wide open and our home is flooded with soldiers.

I scoop Kubuś into my arms.

A heavy Gestapo man in a black leather jacket pushes us aside to stand in the middle of the room, while the evil man remains seated at the table, glaring at us.

The Gestapo man questions Tata in perfect Polish. "Tell me, Doctor Odwaga, when did you last see your son?" I can't help but think he must be a Volksdeutscher.

"Over a year ago," Tata says, looking him in the eye.

"And you haven't heard from him since then?"

"Correct."

"You are lying, you old fool!" A look of rage flashes over his monstrous face. "I won't ask again." He shifts his gaze to Mama and then to me. The way he scans me with his small eyes makes me feel like a ring of kielbasa on the black market.

"You have a beautiful daughter, Doctor. Don't you care what happens to her?"

When Tata doesn't answer, he turns to the other man at the table and speaks in crisp German about taking us to the Pawiak Prison. The man tells him to continue the interrogation, so he takes a step toward me and presses his gun to the back of Kubuś's head. "Tell me where Mateusz Odwaga is, or this boy will be dead in thirty seconds."

Too paralyzed to move, I hug Kubuś tighter, unable to control my shaking body. My mind is racing. I will shield him the moment the bastard intends to fire his gun, so the bullet will hit me instead.

"Please, don't hurt them. We don't know where our son is," Tata says, desperation in his voice.

"Please, Officer, I beg you—" Mama bursts into tears and drops to her knees, placing her head at his feet.

He doesn't pay her the slightest bit of attention and cocks the gun, then begins counting. "Five, four, three—"

A sudden gunshot roars, and he sways and crumples down, blood spilling out from his mouth and running through our creamy Persian rug, like the Vistula through Warsaw.

I'm so shocked that the only thing I feel is the adrenalin shooting through my system. And then I gasp at the sight of Tata holding a small revolver in his hand. I want to run toward him, but something is stopping me from making the slightest motion. I'm more afraid with every passing second, and it's only when my father is shot in the chest by the man at the table that I utter a broken sound. My heart aches like never before.

"Tata! No!" I lunge toward him, but Mama is already embracing him, his head on her lap. Tata's eyes are open. He focuses on Mama and mumbles, "I'm sorry."

I put Kubuś down and snatch off my cardigan, tie it in a knot, and press it to Tata's chest, as if that could help him. Dazed, I anticipate they will pull us away at any moment. Tata's killer now stands to our right. His mouth folds in a sarcastic smile as he snarls at us. It's obvious he's taking pleasure in our tragedy.

Tata moves his gentle gaze to me. "*Kocham*, I love—"

I grab his hand, but he is already gone.

Mama kisses Tata's face all over and sobs with hysteria, repeating over and over, "Don't leave me!"

I cover my face with my hands, stained with Tata's blood, and weep. I feel Kubuś's hand on my arm, but I'm in shock and can't move to hug him.

One of the soldiers says in German, "Are we killing or arresting these women?"

"The old fool is useless now. Just like that bitch and her scared little bunny. No point to waste bullets on them," the bastard says and glares at me with satisfaction and disgust, a handful of soldiers next to him. "Leave them to suffer here. The fool only managed to kill that lard-arse who wasn't even a true German."

He walks away, stops next to the grand piano in the corner, and points to the wall. "Take this sunflower painting instead. Even a replica Van Gogh deserves a better place than this pigpen."

While his soldier removes the painting off the wall, he sits at the piano and puts his fingers on the keys. Those are the same keys Tata touched every day. My chest hurts as if it was just hit by a sledgehammer.

When I hear him play Beethoven's *Moonlight Sonata*, something good dies in me. I stare at my blood-stained hands and then at the devil who's playing Tata's piano. And as the cuckoo clock announces another hour, I vow to myself that one day, I will kill the monster.

3

Finn

Two weeks earlier

OFFICE OF STRATEGIC *Services (OSS) Headquarters, Washington, DC*

I step into a spacious, carpeted office with a mahogany desk and a large wall map. Through the window, the DC skyline shimmers in the afternoon sun.

A gray-haired man walks around the desk and extends his hand toward me. It is my first encounter with Colonel Howard, one of the most crucial people in OSS.

"Captain Keller." He fixes his warm green eyes upon me, then motions toward a chair. "Please sit."

"Thank you, sir."

He walks back around the desk and settles his tall, slim body into a black leather chair. "Would you like anything to drink?" he asks, his tone civil.

"I'm fine, thank you."

"All right then, let's talk business." He smiles for a moment longer and then puts on his wire-rimmed glasses.

His friendly attitude makes me feel more at ease.

"From what I've found in here," he says and points to a paper file on his desk, "and from what I've heard, it's clear that you're one of our best agents."

"I do what's necessary, sir." I'm sure he didn't summon me here to try to boost my self-esteem. Hopefully, he doesn't need me for another European mission. I returned from Greece not even a week ago and didn't expect them to recall me so early.

He leans back in the chair and settles his eyes on me. "You remind me of your grandfather. I have great respect for him. How's he?"

"Busy with his law firm," I say and smile. "Thanks for asking." My grandpa and the colonel fought together in the Great War, but I wasn't aware they knew each other so well.

He nods. "You've a degree from a law school, too, is that right?"

Is he testing me? "I'm afraid not. I still have a year to complete. There're more urgent things to take care of right now."

"You're a true patriot, son." It seems as though he chooses his next words with caution. "Your father was a lawyer, too." His eyes reflect a mixture of compassion and curiosity. "Please accept my deepest condolences."

I feel a sudden heat in my face. "Thank you, but, as you can imagine, I feel rather ashamed when it comes to my father." I hate calling that monster *my father*.

"I don't blame you, son," Colonel Howard says and then sighs. "I learned he had been one of Hitler's most trusted advisers. As a lawyer, he had tremendous opportunities, so it's a shame he got brainwashed by this sick ideology."

"My father sold his soul to a devil." At the thought of him

shooting his brains out, I feel an uncomfortable tightening in my chest and a gnawing surge of nausea forming in my gut. Sometimes, I wonder if it was just madness that brought him to suicide, or maybe repentance. Either way, I don't care.

"So sorry." He has a sympathetic look on his face. "Have you been in contact with your brother?"

"No, not for the past eleven years. He never replied to our letters." Why is he asking all these questions about my family? Does he think I'm a Nazi spy?

"I want to assure you that we do trust you, Captain. You've proved yourself enough, and your family here in America is most respected," he says, making me wonder if he can read my mind.

"I appreciate that, sir."

"What do you know about your brother and his involvement in the war?" the colonel asks.

"Only that he also joined the Nazis and was deployed somewhere in Europe," I say. At his mention of my brother, I swallow hard, then pinch my lips shut. The last thing I want to discuss is Stefan's disgraceful actions.

"In Poland. He is a significant figure in the Gestapo Headquarters in Warsaw." He pauses, his green eyes peering into mine. The air in the room grows heavy. "He works directly under SS-Obersturmbannführer Arthur Veicht in a department that concentrates on eliminating the Polish resistance. Before that, your brother greatly contributed to the mass murders of Polish Jews, and he still hunts down Jews in hiding. Poles call him 'Ruthless Stefan.'"

A cold shiver runs up and down my spine. "I had no idea." My voice sounds shaky, even to my ears. I know Stefan is capable of the worst—but mass murders? I refuse to believe it. But then, deep within, I know this is the truth. I always had in me this desperate need to defend my brother every time he did something terrible. That was a long time ago, though; now we are grown men. He chose to be a murderer.

"Are you okay?" A flicker of understanding shines in his almond-shaped eyes. He stands up and reaches to the side table to retrieve a bottle of scotch and a glass. "Here, drink this."

I take the glass with the liquor, unable to stop my hand from trembling, and finish it in one gulp. I feel an instant burning sensation in my throat and soothing warmth settling in my veins.

"Thank you. Please continue, sir." Uncontrolled anger washes over me. I'm damn tired of apologizing for my family as if that would change anything anyway.

"*Armia Krajowa*, the Polish resistance group, has been watching Veicht for a very long time now. They haven't been able to find a way to liquidate him, though. Veicht is a snake." He pauses, his face looking hard. "But they have found a way to eliminate Stefan."

A lump forms in my throat. "Have they—"

"No, not yet. But they will, and soon. Still, that won't solve the problem because Berlin will send another criminal in his place." His eyes search my face. "There is another way. There is a lot to gain if you step into his place, Captain."

I can't believe his words. "Step into his place?"

"Yes. You're identical twins. Once he is captured by the resistance, you would immediately take his place. You would pass any information you lay your eyes on to the resistance." He studies me, as if trying to determine if I would do it. "Listen, son. I know it's not a good thing when agents are personally involved in their cases, and believe me, if there were any other way, I would not ask you. You don't need to answer right away. Take some time to think and come back tomorrow."

"No need to wait, sir. I've already made my mind up. You see, nothing is going to change the fact that he is my brother, but I'm disgusted by his actions and the stand he's taken. The sorrow that I feel for the innocent people he murdered will stay in me forever. I'm determined to do anything in my power to make amends for at least some of his atrocities." Soreness in my throat and lungs makes me cease talking for a moment. "I will replace Stefan, but on the condition that his life is spared and he is instead imprisoned. I owe my mother that much."

"I will do what I can," he says in a low voice. He clears his throat. "That's all I can promise you."

"Thank you." I'm grateful there is not a trace of pity in his eyes. "When do you need me to leave?"

"In about two weeks. We'll drop you in at night, somewhere in the woods. Local partisans will sneak you into Warsaw, where you'll find the safe house and wait." He stands up and walks around his desk. "All right, that's enough for today."

We exchange a handshake.

"One more thing, Captain. No one can learn of this mission, not even your mother or grandfather."

I swallow hard. "I understand, sir."

4

Finn

1 April 1944

KAMPINOS FOREST, fourteen kilometers west of Warsaw, Poland

They drop me at dawn into a dense woodland filled with soaring pine trees—no sign of a partisan. Without wasting a moment, I dig a hole in the ground and bury my parachute. Sensing someone is observing me, I take my pistol from its holster and sit down. I'm in no rush, so I wait for whoever is watching to appear. In addition to the pistol, I'm carrying a set of forged papers, a map, and a compass. I'm wearing the tattered and rumpled clothes of a laborer—a khaki jacket and flannel trousers.

From a chilly night, it turns to a mild day as the sun mounts toward its zenith. The crisp air smells clean, and rich with pine needles. I listen to a chorus of high-pitched warbling noises in the distance.

"Green frogs like to eat worms for breakfast," comes a male

voice speaking in Polish from behind a tree. It's the coded message I expected.

Breathing a sigh of relief, I stand and reply, "Some of them feed on snakes, too." I'm fluent in Polish, thanks to Pani Ela, who took care of my brother and me while our mother was busy with her acting career. Later, Pani Ela moved with us to America, and thanks to her, I never lost contact with this language.

I see an older man in shabby clothes with a dingy, thick mustache and gray hair hanging from his charcoal cap. Is the Polish resistance short on people? In truth, I didn't expect to see a man my grandpa's age.

"Welcome on Polish soil, son," he says, extending his calloused hand. "I'm Ignacy. Follow me, will you?"

For the next fifteen minutes, we walk through this forestland filled with more pine, oak, maple, and birch, plenty of marshy areas, and dunes. We cross a meadow and a dirt road, and approach a vehicle hidden behind a cluster of willow trees, except it isn't a car. A reddish-brown horse hitched to a long wooden wagon glances at me with his laterally-placed eyes while chewing grass. I suppress a laugh. Poles are damn good at camouflage, aren't they? I learned during my training that Germans forbid civilians in Warsaw from driving cars. Still, I also learned that the resistance breaks those rules whenever they need to, mostly during actions against the occupiers.

When we settle on the wagon's front bench, the man raises a pipe to his mouth and strikes a match. I pull out my pocket map and unfold it.

The man leans forward and places his finger to a position on the map. "We are here, near the village called Laski. We will take this road along the shore of *Wisła*. Vistula." He moves his finger along the river. "All the way here to Adam Mickiewicz Street in Żoliborz." He takes a series of slow and steady puffs from his pipe. "From there, you make it on foot down to Bonifaterska Street, and then to Długa Street and your location."

"I see. How long is the walk?" I take an instant liking to the man.

"No more than thirty-five minutes," he says and snaps the reins. "*Wio*, Gniada." The horse obeys his gentle command.

I fold my map and put it away. We move at a steady pace.

"Do people like to hunt here? I mean, in the Kampinos Forest?" I ask, estimating it would take us over an hour to reach our destination. According to the map, we have fourteen kilometers to go, unless a German patrol stops us. I shiver.

"Always. Even in the seventeenth century, King Jan III Sobieski liked to hunt here. And so did Stanislaw August Poniatowski, our last king," he says and pauses for a short moment, as if trying to recall something. "Are you familiar with Chopin's music?"

"Yes, my mother loves it."

His brown eyes brighten at my words, a glimmer of pride in there. "Your mama has good taste, boy." He pats me on the back and smiles with content.

"She only likes music made by geniuses," I say and smile back.

He breaks into a laugh. "So, you'd probably like to know that the birthplace of Chopin is not far from here, in Żelazowa Wola." He pauses, then adds, "He was one of us, to the end."

"I know his story." We exchange a glimpse of understanding.

"Whoever taught you Polish did a good job."

"Thank you, sir."

He nods with an absent look. "My cousin lives in a village, Palmiry, around fifteen kilometers west from here. He told me that at the beginning, *Germans* picked a forest a few kilometers from there for mass executions. They killed our teachers, lawyers, engineers, senators, artists, politicians, sportsmen—the intellectual flowers of our country. They had done it in secret, but people hear things," he says, his voice trailing off into silence. With his shoulders drooping, he reminds me of a defeated warrior on a battlefield. "People say that's probably where the mayor of Warsaw, Stefan Starzyński, perished. He was our inspiration, the first seed of resistance in us." He sighs.

"Hitler is losing heavily right now. Soon we will put an end to this war," I say, trying to sound hopeful. But there is one horrific truth I can't deny—the inevitable loss of millions of innocent people. If only this man knew that my own family contributed to such slaughters. I feel ashamed, even though I had nothing to do with the acts my father and my brother committed. But here I am, still trying to protect the "Ruthless Stefan" from a death sentence. I pray he might reach a point in his isolated life when he understands the full extent of his deeds and then lives with that crushing knowledge for the rest of his life.

"*Kurwa mać.*" Damn it. He points to two gray-uniformed soldiers armed with rifles, standing next to a small canvas-covered truck, still at a far distance from us. I feel my spine straighten in alertness.

"I didn't expect them here, but they will let us pass as I have a permit to deliver flour to their bakery in Żoliborz," he says with a calm voice.

"Tell them I'm your laborer," I say.

He nods and looks up. "It's going to be another rainy day," he says aloud. The sky is full of dark and ragged clouds.

"Halt!" A tall soldier in a steel helmet shuffles toward us, a rifle ready in his hands.

The older man pulls in the reins. "*Prrry, Prrry.*" The horse obeys his command this time too.

The German soldier scans our faces with his bloodshot eyes. He doesn't blink. "What do you have here?" He points with his weapon to the back of the wagon.

"*Guten tag,*" Ignacy says in accented German, and hands the soldier his permit. "*Mehl.*" Flour. I suspect he only knows a few words in this language.

After examining the papers for a brief moment, the soldier gives them back to Ignacy and glares at me. "And you?"

"*Arbeiter,*" the Polish man says and claps my back. Laborer.

I keep my eyes down.

"Look at me, you Polish swine!" A flicker of irritation and impatience glints in his eyes. "Do you have a *Kennkarte?*" His red nose, puffy lips, and ashen skin give a sickening look to his face.

"Yes." I reach into the inside pocket of my jacket to retrieve the papers. "I'm helping this old man."

He studies them for a long minute, shooting glances at me. I avoid direct eye contact with him while I make a plan in what order I will kill the two of them if there proves to be no alternative. Only woods surround us, and we are still far from Warsaw, so there should be no other patrol near.

"Get down for searching," he says, nudging my arm with his rifle.

I obey, while Ignacy says in a calm voice, "*Arbeiter, meine Arbeiter.*" He holds out a one-liter glass bottle. "Rye vodka. *Gut* vodka." That gets the soldier's immediate attention.

I remain still while peering at the other soldier who's standing a few steps away. He looks to be no more than sixteen; his face is still covered with acne. He must be inexperienced.

The soldier reaches for the vodka and hands it to the younger one, instructing him to bring it to their truck. Then he points his weapon back at me. "*Hande hoch.*" Hands up.

"But, Officer—"

At the sound of Ignacy's polite voice, he turns toward him, glaring. *"Raus,* Get out, you old fool—"

The second his attention is taken by Ignacy, and the other soldier walks away with the vodka, I snatch my pistol out, adrenaline surging through my veins. *Thunk!* I knock him out by striking the back of this head with my pistol.

A split second later, I aim my gun at the other soldier but he just stands there, motionless, with his eyes wide open and hands down. Perfect. Exactly as I expected.

"Toss away your weapon and raise your hands," I say to him in German, and when he complies, I bend down to pick up the rifle beside the unconscious soldier. I throw it to Ignacy, who is speaking out loud to calm down the horse. "Find something to tie his hands and legs with."

"Please don't kill me." The other soldier's voice sounds strained, and he trembles with fear.

"Your uniform tells me you are up to no good." I pick up his rifle. He is still a child—what a shame.

"My parents are dead. I have nowhere else to go," he says in a quiet voice, his head drooping.

"What's your name?" My grandpa told me a long time ago that eyes are the route to a human's soul, and if observed, they can reveal all. This boy's eyes speak not only of fear, but of sorrow. A lost sheep within a pack of wolves?

"Manfred Lange." His lips tremble.

"Manfred, I will have to tie your hands, so you can peacefully wait in your truck."

I press my pistol to his forehead, now beaded with moisture. "Any attempt to rat us out, and I will make sure to find you. Understood?"

"Yes, sir."

After tying the hands and legs of both soldiers, we are on our way again.

"Nice try with the vodka," I say, feeling hollowed out. I hate this goddamned war.

The older man wipes sweat off his forehead. "I swear it did work before. He was stubborn." He studies my face. "He wouldn't let you go."

I nod, but change the subject. "Why do you bring flour to them?"

"They won't get any of it." He winks at me. "I will distribute it among our people."

"So, that permit...." This man continues to impress me with his cleverness. Are all Poles like this?

"Yup. But to our misfortune, Hitler has been enforcing food contingents on us from July to December, when we're supposed to give away sixty percent of our harvest."

"And if you don't?"

"Harsh penalties. Even death," he says.

* * *

I'm still thinking about Ignacy after we part a half hour later. He told me to find him in his village, Laski, if I ever needed his help. I thanked him and wished good luck, but I hope our paths will not cross again. He's much safer far away from me.

As he advised, I walk down Adam Mickiewicz Street. Black clouds cover the sky, and I feel a refreshing touch of drizzling rain on my skin. The district I'm in has many white villas and one-family houses set among large trees in early bloom. People in tattered clothes walk the streets with their heads down. I avoid any German patrols. It's crucial to stay in hiding for the next couple of days until my mission begins.

As I near my destination, the streets become less crowded, as if something has scared people away. I watch tired faces and listen as I keep moving forward. I overhear a man whisper to a woman, "Roundup on Świętojańska."

I'm near my safe house. I just need to look for Długa Street and a gray tenement with a sign for "Café Anna." Just as I'm passing a small kiosk covered with posters, I catch a glimpse of a young woman's face covered with pure terror. A little boy holds her hand. I halt to glance at the posters, to understand what put this fragile blonde in a tattered overcoat into such misery.

She turns my way and bumps into me, dropping a package to the ground. We bend down simultaneously, and when my hand lands on it first, she raises her head. Her stormy blue eyes mesmerize me. I've never seen anyone so beautiful. There is something natural and exciting about her that makes my heart jump like crazy. After she thanks me, without thinking I tell her my name and can't stop myself from kissing her hand. Her name is Irena.

I want to ask her where I can find her, but she rushes away. Are all Polish women so damn pretty?

But then, it dawns on me that I just made a terrible mistake by telling my real name to a stranger. What is wrong with me? Something like that has never happened to me before. I have this strict rule to avoid any romantic endeavors during my missions, and this is the first time I was ready to break it. It's as if she put me in a sort of daze, when all logical thinking ceased to exist. I can't stop myself from staring at her as she slowly disappears from my view.

* * *

By my fourth day in Warsaw, I've grown impatient from being confined in a small room above Café Anna. Finally, near midnight, I hear a knock on the door—three knocks indicate

Anna. But when the rusty door swings wide open, I see a solid figure of a man with an oil lamp held in his right hand and a paper file in the left. He centers the light on the table near the window where I'm sitting and extends his hand. "Call me Witek." He smiles and settles into the other chair. The first thing I notice about him is his broad forehead. He looks to be in his early fifties.

"Good to have you here." He snatches something from his pocket. "Cigarette?"

"No, thanks. I don't smoke."

He lights his cigarette, exhales a cloud of smoke, and says, "Ruined aircraft, sunken U-boats, and wrecked trains. The Germans have their hands full with you." He grins.

I make a dismissive noise. "You Poles have your own people to praise. Have you heard about Agent One?"

The man gives me a long look. "Jerzy Iwanow-Szajnowicz." His voice trails off as he runs a large hand through his thick brown hair. He creases his forehead. "The man was worth an entire division of soldiers." His voice softens. "Gone way too soon." He scans my face, a glint of pain in his gray eyes. "You knew him?"

"I met him on my mission in Greece. He continues to be my inspiration."

"Good, good. You will need much of it for this mission." He is silent for a minute and then continues. "There is a lot I need to tell you before you put on your brother's uniform. How much do you know already?"

"Tell me everything."

"All right then, my boy. You speak Polish well. Does that mean your brother speaks it too?"

"He does," I say and shift in my chair.

He nods. "I'm surprised your father allowed it."

"There was a time when he was different." I feel a thickness in my throat. My parents met in Berlin, where my mother—a famous American actress—had traveled to star in her new film. She fell in love with an ambitious German lawyer, whom she married only a month later. The first years of their marriage were happy, and soon my twin brother Stefan and I were born. But our fairytale ended once my father devoted himself to Hitler and his National Socialism. The thought of it brings a bitter taste to my mouth.

"It's sad how many people have been brainwashed by Hitler's sick ideology." He sighs.

"Way too many," I say, thinking of my parents. Offended by my mother's disapproval and lack of support, my father told her he was in love with another woman. He filed for divorce and demanded Stefan stayed with him. At that point, my relationship with my brother was failing, and I was glad to go with my mom, just as Stefan was glad to stay. I despised my father, for he had been physically abusing my mother for years. The judge ruled in his favor. So, one night when my father was out celebrating with party members, my mother and I left for New York, where my grandparents lived.

"Your brother, SS-Hauptsturmführer Stefan Keller, reports directly to SS-Obersturmbannführer Arthur Veicht, who runs Security Service in Warsaw," the Polish man says. "SD resides on the third floor in the building on Szucha, from which Veicht issues orders to the Gestapo—they are on the first and second floors—to perform actions against the Polish underground."

He stands up, takes the lamp, and leaves the room but returns a minute later with vodka and two glasses. He fills both glasses and hands one to me.

"*Na zdrowie!*" he says. Cheers. The vodka burns my throat, and I feel a warmth spreading throughout my body.

"We are sure Keller lays his eyes on many of those orders before they go to the Gestapo. Keller likes to make an extra 'effort' to go and supervise some of the actions." It seems as though he meditates on what to say next. "We call him 'Ruthless Stefan.'" He gives me a sympathetic look. "Veicht's daughter Gerda is in love with Keller. You must be careful with her—she denounced her own mother." He picks up a paper file from the table, urgency flickering in his eyes. "Here you have the important information and addresses for Keller—read it, memorize it, and destroy it. It had taken a long time to gather it, so you should have most of the details you will need."

He lights his cigarette and, after exhaling a cloud of smoke through his nose, continues. "At the beginning of 1943, Keller moved to a nice villa in Mokotów District, and to our benefit, instead of evicting the villa's owner, he made her his cook. Zuzanna is in her seventies. She will be helpful to you, especially at the beginning."

"How much does she know?" I ask.

"We decided it would benefit you if she knew the truth. You can trust her," he says and takes a drag from his cigarette.

"I don't trust anyone." I fix my eyes upon him.

"You are right, but I trust her. And I advise you do the same." A flicker of impatience shines in his eyes. "For safety, the only other people you should trust here are myself and Anna, and we are going to be your only contacts. We will be sending you messages through a rickshaw boy with red hair and freckles. Our meeting point will be here, at Café Anna."

I nod. "I assume you've already captured him, since you are here?"

"Keller likes to visit a brothel in the city center, and that's where we took him," he says. "One of our girls added a sleeping pill to his drink. He passed out in her bed."

"You know the terms, right?" I ask, feeling a pulse in my throat.

"I do. In the morning, we will have him on the way to London."

"I would like to see him, sir." I rise from my seat. "Even if he is not awake yet."

He holds my eyes for a long moment. "I advise against it."

An awkward silence stretches between us.

"Okay. It must be brief, though. You should be on your way to his villa soon," he says and snatches the lamp from the table and motions for me to follow.

* * *

That night, eleven years ago, despite it all, my mother decided to take my brother with us, but he refused to go. When she tried to force him, he attacked her with a kitchen knife—just like another time when he was little. I stopped him from hurting her, but it broke my mother's heart to leave him behind. He was only fifteen.

Now my brother is propped against the wall in the basement's darkroom, his hands and legs tied with rope. I can't believe how alike we look as grown men in the dim light of the oil lamp. He has the same wheat blond hair and slim build as mine, and we both are medium height, as our father had been. My breath slows as the memories of our shared childhood surface.

His gray eyes blaze into mine, and the amount of hate and emptiness strikes me, almost as if there is no way to get through to him.

"Why are you here?" he asks in German, the language we spoke to each other as kids. A mask of reserve covers his face.

"I want to help you," I say. My brother is just a stranger now.

He tilts his head back and breaks into a malicious laugh, but then his mouth hardens. "It's too late for me—I was cursed the day that bitch abandoned me. Soon, I will join that monster we called 'Father' in Hell." He spits to the floor. "Those Polish sub-humans got me, after all."

Playing games as always. "You know damn well our mother fought for you to the end."

"That's a lie. She ran away with her tail between her legs." His voice is low.

"Damn it, Stefan! You broke her heart and she hasn't been herself since." I regret coming here because I don't know how to talk to him anymore.

He is silent, but there is no confusion or empathy in his eyes.

I feel cold all over. "You kept sending our letters back."

"I didn't need your damn letters. How did you find me here?"

"It doesn't matter. You have done terrible things, brother. Why?" I want him to tell me that he hasn't done any of the atrocities, but I know better. I hate this painful sadness that I can't get rid of. This gnawing feeling of powerlessness. Something went wrong along the way, and since then, my brother has become a monster.

"Help me escape." A challenging look in his eyes. "Prove your brotherly love."

"I can't save you this time—you have to pay for your crimes. You murdered innocent people, goddammit." I feel like we are back to our childhood, and I am confronting him after one of his bad deeds. But this time he deserves a death sentence, and from the way he's behaving, it's clear he's expecting one. "What's your conscience telling you? Do you even have one?"

He spits in my face, his eyes filled with violence. "Get out!"

5

Gerda

4 April 1944

Dear Mutti,

Today marks one year since we last saw each other. Can you believe, Mutti, that I'll be eighteen tomorrow?

Please forgive me for the long silence. I've been so busy settling in here. Papa ordered me to move to Poland a week after the Gestapo took you away. Life here is so different from the life in Berlin. Warsaw is a primitive city. The streets swarm with people dressed in rags. Yes, Mutti—filthy rags. Every time I look at those sub-humans, I restrain myself from vomiting.

Papa says that Führer has it all planned out and that we're in the successful process of the necessary cleansings so we can relieve ourselves of any undesirables.

One night, after many glasses of brandy, he talked about cleansings in the ghetto, overloaded furnaces in some place called Auschwitz, and the need to get rid of the resistance, or something like that. I only pretended to listen, as I found myself engrossed by more important thoughts.

I'm so excited to inform you, Mutti, that I'm engaged. His name is Stefan, and he's so handsome. I met him at a banquet at Hotel Europejski a couple of months ago. Papa is very pleased with his work ethic, and I can see he has a soft spot for him.

Yesterday, I was taken aback by his generosity when he gave me a beautiful sunflower painting. He says it's one of the best replicas of Van Gogh's. I've never heard of that artist, but I like the artwork, as it reminds me of Grandma's garden.

Oh, Mutti, I can't stop thinking of Stefan. I imagine being back in Berlin, married, and enjoying our children. Führer says that a woman's rightful place is at home, as a good wife and mother. I agree with him—I can't imagine anything else that would fulfill me more.

I want to be like Frau Wolf, who is so devoted to her husband. When Herr Wolf moved to Poland, she followed him without a second thought.

I enjoy spending time with her daughter, Inga, who's only a year younger than me and has long, blonde hair and blue eyes, so we look alike. Thanks to her, I don't feel so lonely when Papa and Stefan are at work. Wolf's family moved to Warsaw only a couple of weeks ago. Before that, Herr Wolf supervised a labor camp for Poles who are dangerous criminals. Anyway, Inga said it was so boring there, except the evenings when they sat on their balcony, from which they could oversee the camp and take turns firing their rifle at laboring prisoners. What entertainment, but at the same time, some contribution to eliminating those animals.

I often think of you, Mutti, even though it's so painful to know that you betrayed Führer.

I know I did the right thing, and please be assured that I did it only to protect you.

Papa forbade me from contacting you, but I miss you, so I sneaked into his study and found your file, and I know that you are at

*the women's correctional facility called Ravensbrück. I hope they
have been keeping you comfortable over there and that my letter finds
you well.*

*I trust that Papa will one day forgive you and understand that
you regret your terrible sin. You do regret it, Mutti, right?*

I'm looking forward to your letter.

Your only daughter,

Gerda

"GERDA?" She hears her father's voice as he enters the room.

She folds the letter to Mutti and places it inside her book.

"Hello, Papa. How was your day?"

"Busy as always." He walks toward the liquor without even
a glance at her. He always drinks brandy when he gets home
from work. Most nights, he drinks himself to sleep on the sofa,
and then Gerda has to call the housekeeper to help her bring
him to his bedroom. He is furious if he wakes up not in his bed
the next morning. The last thing Gerda needs is his fury.

"I believe the dinner is ready. Let me check." They never
talk much when he is sober. But when he gets drunk, he mostly
talks about his work projects. He sends reports to the Führer
about his accomplishments, including his contributions to
eliminating the ghetto.

Gerda is proud of her father, and since her teenage years, he
has been her role model. But it is her mother with whom she
has been comfortable talking about her emotions. With her
father, it feels as if they're work associates with the same goals
to accomplish. Gerda likes that. Her mother never could give
her that because she is simply too weak. Her Papa was born to
be the leader, while Mutti is just the follower.

6

Wanda

Two months later

OUR KITCHEN TABLE LOOKS PRETTY, with a bouquet of purple lilacs in a glass vase set in the middle. Its heady, sweet scent tingles in my nostrils and makes me smile. A net curtain blown by a zephyr brushes my face, and I'm delighted to feel the warmth of morning sun on my skin. I love the freshness of June —the month defined somewhere between spring and summer. These days, Mama likes to leave the kitchen window open, since Kubuś needs as much fresh air as possible.

I hear a familiar mix of rapid footsteps and soft laughter. Our little boy flows to Mama, who leans on a counter cutting black bread. She scoops him into her arms and says, "Good morning, sweetheart. Did you have a good sleep?"

"I dreamt of riding a bike." There is a note of excitement in his voice.

Mama opened up her heart to this little boy, who clings to her with all of his being. It hasn't always been that way. For the first month after Tata's death, she didn't leave her bedroom. She barely touched any of the food I brought her and never looked at me. She blames me for Tata's death.

There is no minute in the day or night that I don't blame myself for it too, but I have been doing what Tata would have wanted me to do—I concentrate on our survival. In my free time, I read stories to Kubuś about his favorite Pooh Bear in the book, *The House at Pooh Corner* by Milne, to bring a hint of normalcy to his life.

"You remember what I told you about riding a bike?" Mama asks, her voice laced with concern.

"I know, it's not safe." His eyes sink, and he sighs.

Tata's way to survive had been to distill and sell moonshine, and that enabled him to put food on our table. Not knowing what else to do, I followed in his footsteps, and once a week, I went to Hale Mirowskie—the black market crowded with smugglers. It's a dangerous place, often troubled by roundups. I exchanged Tata's moonshine for food or money by taking my place in line with other smugglers. I kept repeating in a half-voice, "*Bimber* for sale. High quality." When Anna offered to buy it for her café, my shopping at the black market became less humiliating.

Now, Kubuś sits across from me, a mischievous look in his large blue eyes. He stuffs his mouth with black bread topped with beet-colored marmalade, grinding sawdust between his teeth. The quality of that ersatz product is normal to him, as he doesn't know any better.

"We're going to make honey today from the saw thistles," he says, looking at me with pride. "The ones we picked yesterday from our meadow."

According to this adorable boy, our backyard is a meadow he loves to explore.

"Will you?" I smile at him. "By any chance, did your friend visit this morning?"

He swallows and then says with delight in his voice, "I think this time he drilled a hole in our roof."

"No way." I pretend to believe him.

He giggles. "I tricked you."

"You mischief—one day, I'll get you."

"No, you won't. Can you find a new rock in the Old Town for me today?"

"Sure, sunshine."

"You're going out?" Mama asks with her somber gaze on me.

"We're running out of cash, so I thought I would bring some more bottles to Anna. Do we have enough food for today?"

"We do. I'll make an onion soup."

"Don't wait for me. I'll eat at Anna's."

"Make sure to be back before the curfew. I can't stand the thought of you wandering in the blackout streets full of patrols." Her worried eyes search mine. "I had a bad dream last night."

I feel my own eyes soften as I take in her concern. "I will, Mama."

* * *

With my oversized handbag filled with bottles, each individually wrapped in newspaper, I board a streetcar and sit in the back. Only Germans can occupy the front rows.

I peek out the window. Five years of war have brought poverty, reflected in people's tired appearances—skinny features, gaunt faces, and ragged, patched clothing. I'm lucky Mama uses her sewing machine to modify Tata's suits into dresses for us and outfits for Kubuś. Our dresses are dark and simple but in perfect shape, allowing me to enter places like Café Anna.

I get off in the city center and stroll down a narrow, cobbled alley toward Długa Street. The gray, two-story tenement that has been in Anna's family for decades comes into view. A large black sign is spread across the lower level: Café Anna. The second floor consists of apartments where Anna lives, along with her tenants.

The famous Café Anna welcomes me with its savory aroma and warm air swaddling my skin. The large rectangular room is filled with guests seated at small tables covered by white tablecloths, clouds of whirling smoke above them. Anna's regulars are comprised of Germans, in and out of uniform, and their mistresses; not too many Poles frequent the place.

Anna is half Polish and half German. The fact that her Polish mother inherited the tenement allowed Anna to move here ten years ago when she was in her mid-twenties. She began her acting career in Germany, but she always said that it wasn't until Warsaw that she came to love her profession. Soon after the war started, she opened the café. Her official menu shows only a few permitted entries, but the unofficial one contains many choices. Anna is careful to adhere to the two days to be free from meat. She never gets in trouble, as she is generous when it comes to bribing the German inspectors.

There she is in her sapphire cocktail dress—a tall blonde with blue eyes and a pretty face covered with heavy makeup. She moves between the tables and charms her patrons. But all this is only a game she plays to help the Polish resistance. Anna is a true Pole at heart, but people from outside, unaware of her cover, view her as a traitor.

I make my way through the room and follow Anna into the kitchen. I want to get rid of the moonshine as soon as possible.

Half an hour later, seated at the back table, I listen to Anna play piano and sing Marlene Dietrich's love song, *Lili Marlene*. When she finishes, there is an explosion of applause and cheering. While she bows politely and steps off the stage with the lightness of a feather, a short man with a long nose, dressed in a black tuxedo, brings the piano to life again. Usually, he plays Bach, Beethoven, Wagner, or Mozart for the rest of the evening. This man possesses a rare talent. He doesn't just play the music; his skillful fingers brush through the strings of people's souls with the exquisite tenderness of a master.

I'm looking forward to this remarkable experience. Deep inside, I know this music is the real reason I've come here today.

"I'm impressed you are still here." Anna plops down into the chair across from me and takes a drag from her cigarette. Her eyebrows flow to her hairline in apparent surprise.

Smiling, I gesture toward the stage. "I have this weird craving for good music today."

She doesn't smile back. Instead, she covers my hand with hers and gives me a long look, filled with compassion and kindness, no trace of pity evident there. That gesture speaks more of support than any words could and gives me a strange assurance that I'm not alone with my struggles, after all. Anna has this calming influence on me, and I think of her as my older sister. There is a unique quality about her that I like very much: she directly addresses people and their situations.

"I wish those animals appreciated it as well." She rolls her eyes. "The louder he plays, the louder they talk."

I open my mouth to comment, but the words stop dead in my throat at the sight of a man who stands behind Anna and watches me. An uncontrollable shudder sweeps through my body. It's Tata's murderer. All at once, I yearn for a gun or knife or any weapon that would allow me to kill him. I never knew I was capable of hating someone with such force. Just the sight of him brings me to the verge of screaming. But I'm silent like a fish in this place crowded by people like him. I can't even call them *people*. I can't even call them *animals*. They are worse than barbarians. I want to get up and start throwing things at him, just to release some of the tension from my chest. Instead, I brace myself, ready for his ugly attitude toward me. One thing is for sure—I'm not afraid of him. Not anymore. I would rather die than ever again let him hurt me, because what he did to me is the worst agony one person can inflict on another.

He holds my gaze as if he is trying to find something in it, but soon his face shows only confusion.

"Fräulein Otenhoff." He addresses Anna with a polite smile.

At the sound of his voice, she turns and fixes her mouth into a gentle smile. "Hauptsturmführer Keller." She raises her eyes to his face and, in a pleasant manner, gestures toward an empty chair. "Won't you join us?"

Anna is a skillful actress, so I'm not surprised how quickly she adjusts to his unexpected presence. I decide to follow her suit and put on an act in front of him, too, only to create the opportunity to kill him later.

"Please allow me to introduce you to my dear friend, Wanda. Remember you told me once how you like the still paintings in my café? Well, they came from her brush."

He glances at me with open admiration and says, "Beautiful work."

Great, now he will be removing my paintings from here, too. "Thank you, but I've given up painting," I say, unable to remove the hostility from my tone, even though I'm really trying my best.

He arches his eyebrow. "Why, if I may ask?"

"The war took it away from me," I say. I can't believe he's actually talking to me in a polite manner. But his hurtful words from that one terrible night circle in my head as I feel fury rising within me. I hate playing games.

He ignores my answer. "The piece with dried roses reminds

me of a song my mother likes. Believe it or not, it's a Polish song."

What a fake, cunning man. It upsets me that I can't find a trace of the violence or deadly malice from two months ago in his face. Even though the look of arrogance is still there, he has a more genuine approach, just like the first time I met him. That makes it so much harder for me and confuses me like hell. How can one person behave in such different ways? He is an excellent actor; it is almost as if he has two natures, like Doctor Jekyll and Mister Hyde.

"That's interesting. Why a Polish song?" Anna asks.

"My nanny was Polish, so I got to learn many Polish songs throughout the years."

"Did she teach you to speak the language as well?"

"She did, indeed." For a moment, a callous grin covers his face. "By the way, you can be assured I do appreciate the high-quality music you provide here."

Anna doesn't blush, but she bursts out laughing, then changes the subject. "Actually," she pauses and sighs, "my dear Wanda is in a deep despair, as she has been worrying about her good friend Jan Masialski, who disappeared a year ago." She looks at him with a touch of expectation in her wide blue eyes.

"So sorry to hear that." He glances at me. "Please let me know if I can be of any help."

I'm too stunned to answer, so I pretend to listen to the music. What is she talking about? Who's Jan Masialski?

"I see Adam is taking a break from his piano concert," Anna says, a glimmer of laughter in her eyes. "Would you like to sing for us the piece you just mentioned?"

A teasing smile crosses his face. "Only if Miss Wanda allows me to."

I meet his gaze and feel a flash of anger when his eyes dwell on my lips. I ache to tell him to get his eyes off my face, but instead, I crinkle a fake smile and nod. I hope he sings it in Polish and gets arrested by his Gestapo friends.

When he walks away, I touch Anna's arm and say, trying to control my aggravation, "What were you talking about? Who's Jan Masialski?"

Her eyes hold mine. "Last night, I couldn't sleep, and all at once I had this memory of Mateusz showing his forged *Kennkarte* with that name to the German patrol. Maybe that's why we can't find him. Maybe he used that name to keep you safe while he's under arrest."

"Why did you mention that to this Gestapo man?"

"He might be able to help us."

"He is the last person I would go to." I can't believe she would say such a thing. I have to tell her he is Tata's murderer.

"You are wrong—he is the only person we are safe to ask for help. I can't tell you more, but you have to trust me," she says. There is this assurance in her eyes that makes me speechless. She trusts him. How is it even possible that Anna, who is so good at figuring people out, trusts that skunk?

"Does he come here often?" I ask, trying to hide my confusion.

"Not really." She rises from her seat. "Do you want me to send you some food?"

"No, thanks, but I would like some vodka." I wonder why she is so secretive about him.

"You hate vodka," she says in puzzlement.

"I'm in the mood for it today." I just interacted with Tata's murderer, for God's sake. And now he is about to play the piano again, just like the other night.

She rolls her eyes. "One shot?"

"A whole bottle." If she only knew. I want to confess to her the truth but I can't look her in the face now. It's obvious she likes that man. If I didn't know her so well, I would think she'd turned into a traitor too. But I know that's not the case. I trust her more than I trust myself, but right now I just can't talk of what happened on that tragic night. Maybe soon.

She breaks into a laugh and steps away.

My gut tells me to get up and leave at once, but if I want to find an opportunity to kill him, I have to stay and play my game as he plays his. One thing is sure—I need some help, and vodka seems like a good start. At the sound of the first tune, I yearn to run away, unable to stand this farce anymore. I wish I had a gun, so I could walk toward this bastard at the piano and shoot him. I'm appreciative when the waitress brings my vodka. I drink the first shot in one gulp and experience only a mild cough. The liquid burns along my throat, and the warmth travels through the rest of my body. At the sound of the first lyrics, I knock back the second shot and finally feel the initial sparks of blissful numbness.

To my disappointment, his voice is strong when he sings in German about autumn roses, beloved lips, and hearts.

I consume two more shots of vodka and begin feeling hot and dizzy. Why does this devil have to touch everything that's important to me? It's almost as if he knows that the *Autumn Roses* has always been my favorite song.

Then he sings of goodbyes and fading roses.

My brother's friend, Andrzej Włast, wrote the lyrics for this beautiful piece, and Artur Gold composed the music. They were both Polish Jews sent to the ghetto and then murdered by those criminals. And now, one of the murderers is performing their song in German, just like that. I feel a surge of nausea. I'm unable to listen any longer, so I grab my handbag and walk toward the rear exit.

7

Wanda

ANNA'S tiny courtyard is encircled by a tall stone wall, giving her privacy. A sudden wave of hot air hits my skin, adding to the sickening feeling in my stomach. Another twist of nausea sweeps over me, so I make a desperate move toward a small bucket with water, where Anna has a habit of dumping her cigarette stubs. Why did I have to drink vodka on an empty stomach? After I heave, I feel instant relief, but I can't raise myself upright. It's as if I don't have any control over my body while my mind is still working with the utmost clarity.

I experience a sudden eruption within myself—every pent-up emotion flows out like lava from a volcano. I cover my face with my hands, trying to hold back tears, but I fail. For the first time since Tata's death, I let my guard down and allow myself to cry. For nearly two months, a need for survival overpowered me, so I did what I had to do when Mama closed herself off from the world and Kubuś needed me. But now, it's all surfaced, bringing waves of tears at the thought of Tata's limp body in Mama's embrace while his murderer played *Moonlight*

Sonata. Then he stole the painting I had made for Tata. That single night, he'd managed to rob me of my soul. Now I'm just a lifeless puppet with a heart wrapped in darkness.

At the thought of that monster playing his double game today and acting as if the other night had never happened, another surge of nausea comes over me. I want to put my face in the bucket and suffocate; it's better to die than to be exposed to this world of madness. But someone touches my shoulder and hands me a handkerchief. I take it and try to wipe my face, but floods of tears are still emerging. I'm sure it's Witek—he talked to someone in the kitchen when I made my way here. He's like a father to me, so without opening my eyes, I turn and reach to him for comfort, snuggling my face into his shoulder. Without a single word, he embraces me, making me feel safe and whole. His touch is warm, and it feels just right, the kind of a sensation I haven't experienced for a while. When I raise my head, I feel an instant chill travel down my spine.

I jump back and glare at the man with smoky eyes. My first instinct is to run away, but my common sense wins once more, keeping me rooted to the ground. If I act weird, he can easily shoot or arrest me. I must continue playing the sick game.

"I'm so sorry," I say. "I didn't realize the strength of the vodka."

His face seems to have a serious expression. "You have nothing to apologize for. Let me drive you home."

"Oh, no, please, don't trouble yourself. I'm fine to take a streetcar," I say, praying he believes me.

"It's no trouble."

Play along or run away?

"Wanda, dear, please allow Hauptsturmführer Keller to bring you safely home," Anna says from behind. "You are in no condition to get there by any other means."

A couple of minutes later, he guides me toward a black Mercedes, starts the engine, and asks in a soft voice, "What's your address?"

Why does he ask? Is it possible he doesn't remember me? I wonder how often he goes to people's houses at night, turns their lives upside down, and then spends his days acting like a nice guy. Will the memory come back to him if I tell him my address? I decide to give him a location of a tenement my friend used to live in, a couple of blocks from my home.

"Wilson Square twenty-nine in Żoliborz," I say, and lean back in the leather seat, pressing my right hand to my forehead and closing my eyes. We drive in silence. I trust Anna, who appears not to doubt his intentions. Are they romantically involved? I need to tell her the truth about this man.

I open my eyes—we are approaching the location I gave him. Then the music emerges from a street megaphone on Wilson Square. The powerful sound of the national anthem, "Poland Is Not Yet Lost," comes out of the blue, though I suspect our boys from the resistance are behind it. It's incredible to hear it, and I can only imagine that other Poles who listen to it in their homes or workplaces feel the same, except that the timing isn't the best for me. I'm afraid to look at the man next to me. When I do, he forms his mouth into a half-smile. Maybe he cares about Anna and wants to look good in front of her friends?

"If you want to find out about your friend who disappeared, meet me in the Żeromski Park main entrance on Thursday at four o'clock," he says. He pulls over next to an old apartment building, half-ruined in the 1939 siege. "I can't promise miracles, but I will make a few phone calls."

I nod. "Thank you." I know what I will do when I meet him there. Now, it's also about saving Anna from this psychopath.

To my relief, he drives away before I reach the apartment door. Once the stress dissolves, I walk toward home, battling a fresh wave of nausea. At this point, I need a strong ersatz coffee or anything that will soothe my stomach and my pride.

* * *

Three days later, at four o'clock, I edge toward the Żeromski Park entrance from Wilson Square. I wonder if he will already be there; if not, I will have to wait since the park is not permissible to Poles. It's a warm afternoon with a gloomy sky —how the weather reminds me of my emotionally unstable state. The impending rain works in my favor, as it allows me to wear Tata's hunter green raincoat, with the pockets hidden in its folds.

He stands next to the park entrance, talking to the armed guard. He seems to be relaxed, in his Doctor Jekyll mood again. I feel a quiver in my stomach, and my jaw clenches, but I quickly remind myself to pretend.

"Hello," he says, smiling at me while examining my raincoat. "I wasn't sure if you would make it."

I'm determined to strike up a decent conversation with him this time, but the words fail me again, so I smile.

"Let's find a quiet spot," he says and strides toward the park.

I hurry after him, expecting the guard to grab my arm, but he lets me pass.

"Are you familiar with this place?" he asks as we walk toward a fountain with a sculpture called *Alina*, a young girl wearing a folk dress. In one hand, she's holding a large jug she needs for raspberry picking, while with her other hand, she waves greetings to passersby.

"I am. My family used to like to have Sunday picnics here."

I pause, not sure whether to continue, but the plan is to act friendly. "I learned to ride a bike here."

"Really?" He points out the irregular paths and says, "I suppose if you managed to ride it here, you could do it anywhere else."

I smile. "True." I can still hear my father's patient voice, telling me that Kraków wasn't built in a day every time I fell off my bike.

We perch on a bench and admire the sculpture surrounded by overgrown grass and yew bushes—the park's flora gives way to conifers. I have seen the statue of Alina a million times, but today it's somehow different.

"Do you know the story behind this sculpture?" he asks.

"The sculptor, Henryk Kuny, made it after being inspired by the Polish tragedy tale titled *Balladyna*, written by Juliusz Słowacki in 1834. Alina was the girl murdered by her mean sister Balladyna, who did it to marry a prince and become rich. After she killed her sister, she took her jug filled with raspberries that she needed to win the prince's hand, as she was too lazy to pick her own."

"That sounds like a very entertaining story."

I nod, and when he doesn't look, I dig my nails into my fists. Balladyna is a murderer, just like the man sitting next to me.

"I'm afraid I do not have much news for you," he says, looking at the fountain. "Are you sure the name Fräulein Anna gave me is correct?"

That doesn't sound good. "Yes."

"The only man with that name that I was able to trace died in 1941, so he is not the one you are looking for. But at least now you know your friend might be still alive."

That was the man whose identity Mateusz used, according to Anna, anyway. What a mess.

"Thank you for doing this," I say, putting my hand on Tata's spare revolver in my coat pocket. It's the perfect moment to do it—to kill him now and run to the other entrance of the park. My hand feels limp and sweaty in my pocket. I worry that I'll drop the revolver.

"I take it he means a lot to you?" he asks.

I'm startled by his question. "He is like a brother to me." I finally have a perfect opportunity, so why I can't bring myself to pull the trigger? *It's not how I raised you;* I hear Tata's voice in my head. *I tried to save you, and I succeeded. Don't ruin it; don't succumb to the evil. Get rid of the darkness and spread the light.* I shiver from cold drops of rain on my skin. Is this a sign from Tata?

"We need to leave," he says as a bolt of lightning tears across the sky. A peal of thunder follows.

I arrive home soaking wet but feeling lighter inside, as if someone has taken a heavy load off my heart. I change into dry clothes and watch Mama at our dining table, working on her Singer sewing machine. Kubuś and Jacek are playing a card game, and every time Kubuś uncovers a new card, he yelps in excitement. Jacek's visits bring him so much happiness. He used to come for chemistry and biology lessons with Tata and now spends time with Kubuś. Sometimes, I teach him English.

I walk toward the grand piano—the wall behind it looks empty without the sunflower painting I made for Tata for his seventieth birthday. I sit down at the old piano bench, touch the white-and-black keys, and whisper the sign: "Wm. Knabe and Co. Established 1837."

I miss Tata so much. I strike the first notes of Chopin's *Nocturne in E Flat Major.* Tata loved it most for bringing him the joyful memories of his youthful years when he lived in the country. But Mama slams the keyboard cover on my fingers— the same thing she used to do to Tata when he played the forbidden Chopin.

"Ouch!" I stare at my inflamed fingers. "How could you?" She glares at me without a word.

"Fine." I march off and slam the door behind me, feeling like a teenager again.

8

Finn

"MAKE YOURSELF COMFORTABLE, DARLING," Gerda Veicht says, inviting me into a vintage-style sitting room. "I have to freshen up, and then we can enjoy a cup of coffee." She raises her pale blue eyes and smiles at me.

"Take your time, sweetheart," I say and peck the long-legged blonde on the cheek. Her round face lights up before she struts away. I feel a bitter tang in my mouth. This woman is so amoral and heartless that it scares the hell out of me.

I edge toward an antique sofa and ease myself down onto the rock-hard furniture. Every surface in this house is cold, smooth, and shiny, in contradiction to the outside—the poverty of Warsaw's bloodstained streets.

"What a pleasant surprise," a cold voice breaks in on my thoughts.

I surge to my feet and raise my right arm. "Heil Hitler."

Veicht salutes back and strolls toward me. He reclines into a Victorian walnut armchair on the other side of a low table.

"Can I offer you something stronger to drink?" he asks as a

thin lady with salt-and-pepper hair and a wrinkled face approaches.

"Brandy will do," I say. "Thank you, sir."

He glances at the Polish lady and says, "Karolina, get me brandy and two glasses." With his hooked nose, small eyes, and thin lips, he reminds me of a falcon. Hitler's falcon.

He focuses on me. "So, Hauptsturmführer Keller, how's your evening? Hope you didn't disappoint my daughter?"

I clear my throat. "Not at all, sir. We went to the Theater der Stadt Warshau, as Gerda wanted to see *Der Graf von Luxemburg*."

"Oh, that operetta about love that ends happily ever after." He smirks at me. "Our romantic Gerda." He takes a sip of brandy. "Any issues while you were out?"

"No, not at all, sir," I say, tilting my head back.

"Good. I've decided Gerda will leave for Berlin in August." He shakes his glass and gulps down the rest of the liquor. "I'm concerned about her safety here—those criminals murdered another five of our agents."

I make firm eye contact with him. "I will miss Gerda terribly, but under the circumstances, I agree, she should go back to Berlin."

He nods. "She can start planning for the wedding, and perhaps you can join her there soon." A teasing smile crosses his face. "You lovebirds."

"I'm looking forward to it," I say, raising my glass. Thanks to Witek's papers, I've learned that Stefan and Gerda were already engaged and planned to have a glamorous wedding in Berlin. My brother is not capable of loving anyone, so it was clear he did it for the sake of his career. Being engaged to Gerda didn't stop him from visiting brothels though. I feel a need to spit.

I have no choice but to keep Gerda happy and play along

with it. If the princess becomes upset with me, the old man will not hesitate to send me to the Eastern Front to fight the Soviets.

His face grows serious. "We need to find better ways to deal with those Polish parasites," he says, pausing to refill his glass with brandy. "It disgusts me to even think of that action with their *Biuletyn Informacyjny*." His face becomes livid with anger.

"What action?" I ask, trying to keep my face neutral. What the hell? This idiot is clearly into something evil again.

"I just learned that yesterday, our agents accidentally came upon a location where those bastards print their piece of garbage." He strikes a match and lights up a cigarette.

My heart feels like it's shrinking. "Their journal?" He must be talking about the location on Wawelska Street.

"Yes, if you want to call it that. They were in the middle of printing the twenty-second edition of it." Cigarette smoke emerges from his hooked nose. "One idiot was killed in the shooting with our people, and the other one keeps silent as a lamb." He narrows his eyes. "You know what they have been writing about?"

"Probably nothing good." He's such an idiot.

"Those Polish pigs think that we are nearing the last stage of the war, and soon they will be free," he says, his face shadowed as he lets out a gruff laugh.

"Ridiculous. I suppose they got their courage after the Poles ascended Monte Cassino," I say, rolling my eyes.

He ignores my last comment. "Starting tomorrow, I will work on implementing some drastic changes. We are way too lenient." He pauses and listens. "I hear Gerda's voice, so let's cease this conversation. Just one more thing—I need you in my office tomorrow at nine to discuss a manhunt at Paderewski Park."

"Of course, sir." I should just kill this monster. But I know very well that such an act would not solve things, only complicate them, as Berlin would send a replacement immediately.

Gerda walks in looking wickedly beautiful in her white summer dress. An angel on the outside but truly evil within. The Polish lady follows her, carrying a tray with coffee and strudel. The smoky aroma of coffee travels through my nostrils as I watch Karolina setting the low table with gold-rimmed china.

"Papa, please, no politics tonight," Gerda says after taking her place beside me. "Stefan came over to relax."

Veicht winks at me. "Of course, honey. We were talking about your upcoming wedding." He grimaces as he smiles.

Her eyes flash. "That's much better." Gerda watches Karolina pour coffee into each cup. When she is filling up my cup, her hand unexpectedly trembles, and some of it spills.

"I'm so sorry," she says in a quiet voice, and then she glances at Gerda and winces.

"Not to worry," I say and use my napkin to wipe off the coffee.

But Gerda raises her hand and slaps the poor lady across her face before pushing her away. "Get out, you, stupid woman. Can't do the simplest thing." Her voice shakes with fury.

While Karolina slips away, Gerda finishes filling my cup. She says with a sweet voice, "Darling, you must taste some of the strudel Karolina baked. I love this heavenly taste of apples, almonds, and raisins." As she places a piece on my plate, nausea grips my stomach.

9

Wanda

WE ONLY HAVE sixteen bottles of Tata's moonshine left. Two
more trips to Anna. I may have to accept her offer to become a
portraitist in her café, after all. We need money to buy food.
While in the basement, I find a small book on making vodka, so
I take it with me and walk outside. I'm unable to stay in the
basement too long because of the lingering odor of over-
fermented grain and yeast that reminds me of Tata.

It's a lazy Sunday morning, with gentle sunshine, a blue sky
and fluffy white clouds, the kind of day that makes people
relax. But there are too many worries clouding my mind. I
perch on a rusty wooden bench—Tata made a point to refurbish
it every few years, and he planned to do it this year. To my
right, Mama pulls weeds in her vegetable garden; she makes a
lot of effort to care for it, as it provides extra food throughout
the summer and fall. Until Tata's death, I relied on my parents'
resourcefulness and took it for granted. Why was I so self-
centered?

I scan the book in my hands. No, there is no way I can do
this. My inevitable fate is to draw the ugly faces of the Nazi

murderers. As I toss the book aside, something slips out of it—a picture. When I lift it from the ground, my chest tightens. The photograph shows my father in his late forties, standing with a young woman who looks like my twin sister, but of course, I don't have one. She is pretty in an ivory net-and-lace dress with a sheer drop waist. She's holding a baby in her arms. My mind is racing. Is she one of our relatives on Tata's side?

I proceed through the garden and approach Mama. "I need to show you something," I say, scrutinizing the picture in my hand. "Is she one of our relatives?"

She stretches, slips off her gardening gloves, and wipes the sweat from her forehead. She snatches the photograph from my hand. After glancing at it, a frown clouds her face."Where did you find this?" she asks without meeting my eyes, her voice tense.

I'm surprised by her reaction. There must be something I don't know.

"In Tata's book," I say. "Why? Who is she?"

She closes her eyes as if she's trying to think. "I guess it's time you learned the truth, after all." Her eyes flash open to meet mine. "She is your biological mother," she says in a deep voice that vibrates along my nerves.

My entire body is pulsating to the thump of my heart. "I... I don't understand." I take a step back.

"Your father had an affair with a young nurse." Her eyes fill with tears. "He moved out to live with her and filed for divorce. But a couple of months after you were born, your mother was killed in a car accident."

A lump forms in my throat. "What?" I refuse to accept what she's telling me.

Her face darkens with pain. "Mateusz was only ten, and you needed a mother too, so it was for the best that your father and I remarry."

A sudden wave of anger washes over me. "Why did you hide it from me?"

"Your father believed it was in your best interests," she says, wiping away her tears.

My pulse races. "Now I understand why you hate me."

She winces. "Oh, *kochanie*, darling, no, I don't hate you." A note of pleading creeps into her voice.

I have a desperate need to be left alone, so I bolt away without saying a single word.

* * *

I want to run far away from Mama and home, but being out in the streets for too long is dangerous in my state of mind, so I end up in Anna's flat above her café.

I can't bring myself to talk much about it, so I just tell her what I've learned.

She sits beside me on the sofa with her eyebrows drawn together. Her steady eyes settle directly on me. "I know you are overwhelmed now, but believe me, as time goes by, you will be able to sort things out and come to terms with it," she says and wipes the tears from my cheeks.

I fail to find any comfort in her words, but her empathy touches my soul. "I'm feeling so broken that I can't even gather my thoughts together."

She cradles my face in her hands. "We are at war, Wanda. You can't afford to wallow in self-pity for too long, or you won't survive," she says. "Soldiers don't cry on a battlefield. They move forward. They fight."

The clarity of her thinking sobers my mind. "You are right."

She stands up. "I'm taking you to Łazienki Park. You will find your needed peace over there."

The park and palace complex has been closed to Poles since

the beginning of the war, but Anna can enter it thanks to her German citizenship. I keep my canvas bag of supplies at her place, so we take it with us every time we go to the park. She explains to the guards that I'm her portraitist.

We stroll through alleys, enchanted by trees and bushes, mesmerized by the sudden peace. When we take a trail around a pond, I stop in my tracks, startled by the eerie, high-pitched sound of a crying baby. A tremor shakes my body.

"Don't be fooled by it," Anna says and points to the left, where an enormous peacock spreads its feathers in a rainbow-colored fan.

We break into laughter and continue on our way to an open-air amphitheater on the east bank of the south pond—our favorite place in the park. We sit on a front-row bench in the amphitheater's lowest section, separated from its stage by a narrow strip of a pond. The scene—guarded by a stone monument of a lion—imitates the Roman Forum's ruins. It is quiet despite the deep, trumpeting sounds from the swans in the pond. The sun shines on the water, intensifying the earthy smell of rotting algae and mud.

We don't speak to each other; we rarely do when we come here. Instead, we drift into our thoughts, taking in the combined beauty of nature and the ancient world of the theater on the island. As yet still untouched by the occupiers, this place is an oasis of peace to me. Before the war, I watched Anna in so many great plays staged here, but it wasn't until we Poles were forbidden to come here that I started truly appreciating it and viewing it as my escape from the ugly world.

"Take out the drawing of me," Anna says urgently. "Someone is coming."

I comply right away. There is a woman's laughter in the distance, and soon a couple appears on a trail. My stomach clenches. It's Tata's killer.

"Not again," I say to Anna. Of all the places in Warsaw, he has to come here.

He is accompanied by a tall, pretty blonde who looks like an angel in her white summer dress. Together, they make a striking couple. Is this woman as heartless as her partner?

"Let me do all the talking, and just pretend you are working on the drawing," Anna says. Then a smile lights up her face as she rises from her seat. "What a nice surprise."

"Oh, Fräulein Otenhoff," the woman says. "I'm so glad to meet you here. At least this time, I won't get bored while Stefan contemplates this miserable pile of ruins."

I can't help looking at her, but at the same time, she scowls at me.

"I see you have company."

"I brought my portraitist with me," Anna says, and takes a drawing to hand to the woman. "She is very talented."

"That is a stunning drawing of you." She raises her eyes to Anna and says, "Perhaps we can borrow your portraitist? I would love for Stefan and I to have such a souvenir before we go back to Berlin."

"Absolutely. She can draw your portrait now, of course, if you are available." A wry smile lifts the corners of Anna's lips.

"Please, don't trouble yourselves with this today. We should be heading back soon," the man says, a note of firmness in his voice.

"Nonsense, darling," the round-faced blonde scolds him. "Where should we pose?" she asks, her gaze on Anna. This woman is used to having her way.

"You should climb to the upper level, so Wanda has a good view of you."

I will get you for this, Anna Otenhoff. I flip my drawing notebook to an empty page. Tracing the woman's features comes with ease, but the man's face gives me the most trouble.

When I look at him, I see warm eyes and a soft smile, but I know better. He is a snake.

I sketch his empty, cold stare from that terrible night. The evil look on his face matches her wicked face. And that reflects his true nature. I can't find it in me to make a false portrait of this murderer.

When I finish, the woman moves toward me and snaps the notebook from my hand without a word, glaring at me. But the moment she looks at it, she smiles with delight.

"This is stunning," she says and looks at Anna with gratitude, ignoring me. After she shows it to Anna, she hands it to the man. "Look at it, darling. We make a lovely couple. I'm glad I put on this dress today, as it complements your uniform." She doesn't wait for his reply but instead excuses herself and asks Anna to take a brief walk to discuss something important. Before leaving, Anna gives me a concerned look as though to say, *Will you be okay here by yourself with this man?*

No, I'm not okay. He's the last person on this earth I want to stand next to or talk to, not to mention being left alone with. Why did fate play a joke on me by bringing him in front of me again? I swear that if I had a gun now, I wouldn't hesitate to pull the trigger this time. His very presence awakens me to the awful reality of Tata being gone because of this monster. I snap out of my reverie. If I want to survive this war, after all, I must pretend.

He keeps staring at the sketch with a troubled, almost pained expression, and that's when I know he notices the traces of evil I edged into his eyes. He raises his gaze to me. "Thank you," he says and moves nearer to me. "I'm so sorry for her."

When I nod, he hands the notebook back to me. An electric sensation of his fingers brushes against my skin. I feel confusion in every fiber of my body, but instead of backing off, he gets closer and touches my cheek, caressing it with his palm.

My heartbeat is fast from a combination of fear and excitement. I know it is all wrong and I want to push him away, but, hypnotized by his sensual touch, I can't bring myself to move. At the sound of approaching voices, I snap away from him, and all at once my mind sobers. What came over me? I glance at him, but there is only a glint of pain in his eyes. "I'm not who you think. Trust me," he says, just before stepping away.

* * *

The next morning, I refuse to get out of bed, even when Kubuś informs me that *Ciocia*, Aunt, Krysia came over for a visit. I tell him I have a headache and need another hour to feel better, but he keeps coming to my bedroom every fifteen minutes to check on me. *Ciocia* arrived yesterday after a long trip from Tosaki, a village in northeast Poland, where Tata grew up. But I returned late last night, so I haven't seen her yet.

"Wanda, you must get up." Kubuś peeks from behind the door. "*Ciocia* has a surprise for you."

I'm too paralyzed to do anything. Mama isn't my mother because my father cheated on her. My father—the man I adored so much—abandoned his wife and son for another woman. And despite all of this, Mama took him back when my birth mother died. My birth mother—I look just like her. I will never get to meet her, to know her. The way she holds me in that picture shows her adoration for me. But if she was a decent woman, why did she involve herself in a romance with a married man?

Finally, it all becomes clear—I remind Mama of the woman whom her husband chose over her. This very realization causes a lump to form in my throat.

"I'm sorry, honey. Tell *Ciocia* I will be there soon," I say and smile at my sweet Kubuś.

He seems excited. Most of the time, he behaves like a happy child, despite what he went through. It makes me feel even more ashamed of myself. A wave of nausea squeezes my abdomen when I think of the way Tata's killer looked at me yesterday. I still don't understand why I felt the way I did when he touched me. What was I thinking? Why didn't I run away the moment this evil man neared me? By responding to his touch, I betrayed my father. I betrayed my country. I deserve to have my hair shaved and to be shunned.

He is a manipulative bastard, and I feel nothing more for him than disgust. How can one person have such baffling behavior, though? How can someone with such warm and thoughtful eyes be the same person who murdered Tata in cold blood? His words keep coming back to me: *I'm not who you think. Trust me.*

There is a knock on the door, but instead of answering, I bury my face in a pillow. Kubuś never bothers to knock, so it must be Mama, and I'm not ready to talk to her. But it's *Ciocia's* melodic voice that comes, so I pull the covers down.

"Stay in bed, darling," she says, moving my desk chair beside the bed. "I know how severe headaches can be." She is still the same vigorous woman I remember, but she has aged a lot since I saw her a year ago. War does that to people. Her dark hair, gathered in a bun at the nape of her neck, is covered by thick streaks of gray, and her soft-featured face has many deep wrinkles now.

"I'm so happy to see you, *Ciocia*." I jump off the bed and embrace the lovely lady who is my kindred spirit. I spent every summer during my childhood at her beautiful home in the country, where she lives with Uncle Mirek. She ingrained in me a love for art by teaching me to paint and sketch. She believes I inherited a rare talent from my great-grandmother, Helena.

"Me too, my beautiful girl, me too," she says. It warms my heart to see Tata's deep brown eyes on her face. My father's family was steeped in nobility. Tata grew up in a beautiful manor house where my aged grandparents passed away only a decade ago. *Ciocia* Krysia is his only sibling. Because of his career as a doctor, she stayed in the country to manage the estate. She married, but remained childless.

"How's *Wujek* Mirek?" Now German officers reside in the manor house while my aunt and uncle occupy the gardener's cottage. Uncle Mirek still manages the farm and its workers, but under their rules.

"He's getting by," she says with a sigh. "I'm here to take all of you home from this miserable place." We are used to calling Tosaki our second home, something Tata implanted in us.

I'm not sure if I like what I hear. I'm not ready to move, not now, when something big is about to happen, something that we call *The Uprising*.

"Your mama agrees that you will all be safer with us. What if the Gestapo come back again looking for Mateusz?" She pauses and clears her throat. "What happened to my brother can happen to all of you. It's a miracle they spared you that day." She studies my face with a frown. "I can only imagine what you've been up to, Wanda."

Maybe Mama and Kubuś should move to the country, after all. Once The Uprising starts, I will be too busy to care for them. And who knows how things will go here. I wonder why I didn't think of it earlier. "Thank you." I kiss my aunt's hand and try to stop tears from emerging. "But you must understand that I have to stay here. I heard there would be an uprising soon."

"Oh, I understand, Wanda. I truly understand you. And if

only I were younger. . . " She sighs and then gives me a long and earnest look. "Don't be too hard on your mother, honey. Don't forget she did the right thing by forgiving your father and bringing this family together." She cradles my face in her soft hands. "She loves you, trust me."

Part II

"I can't bring myself to open Stefan's letter. I'm so afraid of the ultimate truth about my brother, and I have a feeling this letter explains it all. As Stefan said, it contains the final answers I need in order to move on with my life." ~Finn Keller

Wanda

THE ODWAGA FAMILY estate in Tosaki lies on the Narew
riverbank. It consists of a white manor house, an enormous
garden, residential buildings for employees, farm outbuildings,
and about 250 hectares of agricultural land. A picturesque
willow lane leads directly to the manor house, which German
officers now occupy. We scamper through the sweetly fragrant
garden, accompanied by the whistle-like sound of a
nightingale, to reach a small cottage hidden in the outskirts
where my aunt and uncle live.

I feel tremendous relief that we encounter no humans on
our way. *Ciocia* Krysia explains that the German soldiers are
mostly out through the day, and the local people work in the
fields. We left Warsaw around seven o'clock this morning, so by
the time we enter the house, it's two fifteen.

I plan to stay for three days and then go back to Warsaw.
Witek instructed me to pick up some weapons from the local
partisans on my way home.

I spend those days walking in the garden and bathing in the
river with Kubuś. Every rock or flower he finds puts a smile on

his face. I feel tightness in my chest every time I think of our upcoming separation. He's a part of our family now, and I feel responsible for him. He's my reason to survive this awful war, so that he's never alone in the world. I wonder if what I'm experiencing is the same thing other mothers do. I didn't give birth to Kubuś, and Mama is the one who spends the most time with him, but there is this special bond between us that formed from the moment he pulled on my coat the day Tata died.

My relationship with Mama is stagnant. She tries to talk to me, but I'm not ready, so I carefully steer the conversations onto other subjects. In truth, I don't blame her for anything. Tata decided to keep my mother's real identity from me. Mama's only fault is that she couldn't bring herself to love me or even pretend when I needed her during my childhood. I have no right to blame her, not after my father betrayed her and not after she forgave him. I just need more time for things to settle.

On the last day, I borrow my aunt's canvas and oil paints and head toward the river, where I stroll through the majestic garden crowded with oak, red-leaf maple, spruce, and elm trees. I pass a green woodpecker, as well as sparrows and jays dancing in the crowns of trees and bushes. Their concerts are breathtaking.

I freeze at the edge of the garden, just as I'm about to step onto the dirt road there are soldiers riding three-wheeled motorcycles. I recognize the handsome man sitting in the passenger seat of the first motorcycle. He is the German captain my aunt told me to avoid at all costs. She said it's dangerous even to make eye contact with him, as he's been known to lose his temper for trivial reasons and to brutally kill local people. He's on a constant hunt for soldiers and civilians who choose to become partisans and who carry on the fight under the Polish Home Army, hiding in the woods.

I stare at the ground, waiting for the motorcycles to pass.

How is it possible that someone with such good looks—tall, dark-haired, and handsome—has such a sadistic personality? Tata was right when he said not to judge a book by its cover.

I cross the road and hurry down the hill through a green field of potatoes to reach a meadow where farmers are raking hay. As I pass, I wave to them and then enter a small forest dominated by willows, poplars, and white coral viburnum bushes. Then I walk through a reedy area overgrown with perennials and full of hovering dragonflies that make a deep humming sound to find a tiny, abandoned beach right on the shore of the Narew River. I use river water to clean the sticky spider webs off my skin. As I spread my blanket on the ground, I try to recall the meaning of dragonflies. I think it's about letting go of whatever holds us down or holds us back. Is this another sign from Tata? Does he want me to let go of my pain and talk to Mama before leaving tomorrow?

It's a sun-drenched day, so I bathe in the river and then work on my painting. An aroma of fish-tainted water and decaying moss tingles my nostrils—the smell of every summer vacation I spent here. I want to capture the natural beauty of the river bathed in a golden hue of the sunlight, but I grow frustrated with my progress.

Hours later, a sudden commotion behind brings me back to reality. A group of soldiers on horseback halt at the edge of the shore. One of them climbs down from a black horse and approaches me. It's the German captain. Adrenaline shoots through my system as my aunt's words come to my mind: *Avoid him at all costs.*

"What are you doing here?" he asks, in sharp German.

My words stick in my throat as I gaze at him.

A flicker of irritation and impatience shines in his eyes. "Don't you know it's already curfew?"

My spine stiffens at his words. "I'm so sorry. I lost track of time as I got so carried away trying to finish my painting." I leap to my feet and reach for my belongings, but his menacing tone of voice stops me.

"Sit down. I'm not done with you," he says, not a vestige of humor showing on his face.

I swallow hard and obey, wondering how to get out of this? At this very moment, I long to be like Anna with her effortless act. I need to show this man that I'm confident and have nothing to worry about. I need to flirt with him like with the other soldiers at checkpoints. But that doesn't come easy to me this time. The suspicious and sharp way this man looks at me tells me that he can't be easily fooled. *Avoid him at all costs.* Why didn't I listen to my aunt and was more careful? How come I didn't realize it has gotten so late? Once more I must pay for my recklessness.

He orders his soldiers to search the nearby woods and squats beside me on the blanket. His eyes search my face and move to the canvas. "You need to tone your colors down." He picks up the brush and works on my painting for several minutes in uncomfortable silence. "Just like this."

He finds the exact shade of yellow I was trying to come up with. My stomach is clenched, but I'm aware I should praise him in hopes of being spared his enmity. "That is perfect. Do you paint?" I try to sound relaxed, even though my inner alarm tingles.

He smiles. Can someone with such a gentle and confident face commit slaughter against another human? Maybe Aunt Krysia pointed out the wrong man to me. I fail to convince myself, unable to push aside the eerie feeling in my gut.

"Not anymore," he says and half-turns to face me. "Have I seen you around recently?"

"I've been visiting for a few days. I'm from Warsaw."

"What do you do there?" A look of suspicion flashes across his face.

"I work in a sewing factory." I compose a neutral voice. "I better be going, as it's getting dark."

He nods. "The woods are flooded with bandits." He gives me a meaningful look. "Have you noticed any suspicious activities during your stay here? We give a large reward to anyone who supplies us with anything worth checking."

I shake my head. I know my aunt and uncle sneak food at night to local partisans in the woods.

"Well, anyone who breaks curfew rules must be punished." A teasing smile clings to his mouth. "Unless you find a way to convince me otherwise." His gaze locks on my lips.

My heart and mind race. If I start to run away, he will kill me. If I refuse him, he will imprison me for breaking the curfew rules, will he not? For such *crimes*, they send people to labor camps or even kill them. The need for survival grows so strong in me that I remain still. He grasps the back of my head with his hand and covers my mouth with his. As a cold shiver runs down my spine, nausea grips my stomach. I feel only disgust for this criminal and for myself for allowing him to kiss me in order to survive.

At the sudden rattle of gunfire from the woods, he springs to his feet, but before turning away, he says, "We will continue later." A sardonic smile clings to his lips as he takes a few seconds to scan me up and down.

Every fiber of my body is taut with hatred. Over my dead body, will he ever touch me again. Once he is out of sight, I gather my belongings and take another way home to avoid meeting him. I know the area well, thanks to the endless wanderings and hide-and-seek games of my childhood.

* * *

The next morning, I'm up at four o'clock. I pack my bag, careful not to wake Mama and Kubuś—we share a bedroom with two small beds. I kiss the little boy's lovely face. "I will miss you so much, my sunshine," I whisper. Then I kiss Mama's forehead. "Stay well, Mama."

I slip through the dark garden and head north toward a train station in Białystok. Following Witek's instructions, I wait at the edge of the birch tree forest at five o'clock, about three kilometers from the manor. Afraid to stay too close to the road, I wade through the tall grass and rest my back against one of the birch trees. My heart hammers in my chest. I can't stand the darkness and this awkward silence.

"Are you afraid of the red foxes?" a voice in the dark murmurs.

My body stiffens. "I'm only a nightingale lost in a birch forest," I say, repeating the coded phrase Witek told me to use once I encountered the partisans.

"Follow me."

My tense body begins to relax as I dash after the giant, broad-shouldered man who leads me farther into the woods. Soon, we approach another partisan sitting beside a bonfire with his back to us.

"The courier from Warsaw is here," the tall man says, moving behind me.

The other man stands up and turns toward me. At a glimpse of his face, my heart fills with joy. "Mateusz." I refuse to believe my brother is standing in front of me.

But he scoops me into his arms. "My little sister. I didn't know you were the courier," he says, a sudden note of concern creeping into his voice.

"I can't believe it's you," I say, cradled in his embrace.

When we are settled beside the bonfire, my brother introduces me to Tomasz, who soon excuses himself to check the area. Thanks to his tact, we have a few minutes alone. There's so much I want to tell him, but it isn't possible to fit it all into such a short period.

I gaze into his eyes. "Do you know?"

"I do. *Ciocia* Krysia told me," he says, with a somber expression on his now-bearded face. He is gaunter than ever.

"Mama is here, and the little boy we've been taking care of. . . " I clear my throat. "I didn't want to bring them here, but *Ciocia* insisted it's safer for them."

"She is right. As long as the Germans need Uncle Mirek to manage the estate, they will leave him alone." He prods the bonfire with a long stick. "Besides, they'll be running away from the Soviets any day now." A confident smile spreads over his face. "You should stay here, as it will take much longer before Warsaw is liberated."

"I have to go back." I sigh. "I hope you are right about the situation here, though. It's enough that I feel guilty for Tata's death. I couldn't bear if anything happened to them, too."

"Nonsense—it wasn't your fault. They came looking for me," he says, throwing the wooden stick away. "After the last action, when I killed that Nazi murderer who was ordering the ghetto executions, Witek decided it was wiser if I disappeared." He leans toward the bonfire to light his cigarette. "But that didn't help after all."

"If I hadn't acted so recklessly and spilled coffee on that Nazi bastard and brought the boy to stay with us. . . " I say in a strained voice.

He exhales a cloud of smoke. "They would have done it even if you didn't spill coffee on him. You are just a human and make mistakes like everyone else, so stop tormenting yourself and let it go. Plus by helping the boy, you did what was right. That's how Tata raised us to be."

His words mean so much to me; they help my broken soul

to breathe. Maybe he is right after all and my action didn't make any difference. I could see in that bastard's eyes that he was there for nothing good from the moment he entered our home.

"I just wish Tata was still alive. I miss him so much and the guilt in me doesn't help at all." I pause, trying to gather my thoughts. "You know, I almost killed Tata's murderer when I met with him in Żeromski Park, but then I heard Tata's voice telling me to save myself from becoming one of those monsters. And when I didn't do it, I felt this lightness, like something heavy lifted off my chest. At that moment, I felt Tata's presence as if he sat right next to me on that bench."

Mateusz wipes my tears off with his hand. "You did the right thing," he says and sighs. "Anyway, if there is anyone to be blamed, it should be me." His voice is so sad that it tugs on my heart.

I touch his cheek and smile. "Tata was proud of you and that you've been fighting for our freedom."

"I know, and that's why I won't stop until we win." He pulls me into a hug. "I've missed you so much, my little sister."

I should be on the way to the train station soon, but I steal for more time as I have a sudden urge to confide more in Mateusz. "Mama told me about my birth mother," I blurt out.

He pulls away from the hug and his mouth falls open for a quick moment. "Tata made me promise not to tell you," he says, and there is a deep note of guilt in his voice.

"His decision was unfair." My chin trembles. "At least now I understand Mama more."

He throws his cigarette into the bonfire and touches my arm. "I remember being jealous of you when you were little because Mama went for stroller walks with you, sang to you, held you in her lap, and kissed you." He gives me a meaningful look. "It wasn't until your teenage years when something disconnected between you two. Maybe you reminded her of your biological mother too much."

I lift my hand to my chest. "So Mama did try to love me."

A brief laugh escapes him. "She loves you, silly. It's just that you haven't been the easiest since your teenage years. Only Tata knew how to get through your stubbornness."

"I wish I could believe you." Footsteps approach us. Lowering my voice, I ask, "Were you angry with Tata? I mean, for leaving you and Mama?"

"I'm far from judging him. I'd give everything, though, to be able to hear his voice again and his annoying laugh. Life is too short and too damn fragile, my little sister."

"Will you go to see Mama soon?" I ask, my voice full of emotion.

"Yes, I will. There is one more thing I need to ask you." He smiles. "How's Anna?"

* * *

The train ride from Białystok to Warsaw feels endless, with more and more people boarding at each stop. Many of them are smuggling products to sell on the black market, like saccharin, flour, or kielbasa. Usually, if conductors are informed about Gestapo waiting at the Warsaw station, they stop the trains ahead of time to let people out. There is no such commotion today, so the train pulls into the final station without obstacles. I walk through the crowd and pause by the clock in front of the station. It's quarter to six, so I have enough time to get home before curfew. But just when I'm about to get on my way, I get distracted by an uproar among people clashing with barking dogs.

A man in an elegant black suit approaches me. "Halt," he says in a harsh tone. I'm already at the gunpoint of a gendarme.

A cold tremor runs through my body. The same thing is happening to other people, so I'm not their only target. But I'm not smuggling food like most of them. My suitcase contains a dozen small pistols hidden among my clothes—what a stroke of bad luck. The station looked so peaceful just minutes ago.

"Your papers," the man in the black suit says, his eyes bleak and his face marked by a long scar across his right cheek.

I hand him my papers, making sure my hand doesn't shake. My knees feel weak.

"What's the reason for your trip?" he asks, without lifting his gaze from my documents.

"Family visit."

He nods. "What's in your suitcase?"

"Clothes and toiletries." My stomach feels rock hard. Please don't check my luggage. Please.

"I see you work in our sewing factory." He doesn't wait for my reply. "Your papers are in order." Just when he folds my documents back, another man in a black suit appears by his side. A sudden chill hits at my core. It's Alfred Kraus.

Alfred moved from Berlin to Warsaw when he was little, as his father worked in the German consulate. He went to the same secondary school as I did. All the girls liked him for his good looks—tall and muscular— and his skill at playing *piłka nożna*, soccer. When I was seventeen, he asked me out. I liked him a lot too, so I agreed. But one day after school, I saw Alfred spitting at Samuel, a Polish-Jewish boy from our school. He pushed him away, calling him "dirty Jew." The same day, I stood him up by not showing up for our date. Later, I learned that Alfred belonged to a nationalist student group financed by German Nazis.

"Wanda Odwaga," Alfred says. A sarcastic smile twists his lips. "Long time no see."

"This lady's name is Irena Malecka," the other man in the black suit says, handing my papers over to Alfred.

"That's interesting." Alfred's piercing blue eyes meet mine, and the amount of hate in them terrifies me. "She looks just like a Polish slut I went to school with."

An overwhelming sensation of dread cripples my body, but I give him a look like I would give a stranger. "You are mistaking me for someone else. My name is Irena Malecka." I've lost a lot of weight since he saw me last, so I hope he believes I'm someone else.

His cold eyes are blazing into mine. "Come on, Wanda. I could not forget you." His gaze wanders down my body and stops at my bag. "Do you still have any of your father's moonshine?" A mocking smile appears on his mouth.

My spine stiffens at his words. My father started making *bimber* only a couple of years ago, long after I saw Alfred last. How does he know it, then? Does he have something to do with the Gestapo coming to our home?

"Search her bag," the Gestapo man with a scar says to the gendarme, a trace of impatience in his voice.

A clutch of panic settles in the pit of my stomach, but it soon transforms into a numb feeling of powerlessness. The gendarme unrolls the first pistol from my pajama dress. Alfred's face beams with satisfaction as he orders to take me away.

11

Finn

AN IRON GATE squeals under my touch. I walk through a dark garden to reach the main entrance of the exquisite villa that I occupy. I pause and listen to the stillness of the night, breathing in crisp air intensified by the sweet fragrance of night-scented stock, pink-and-white flowers that open at night. The crescent moon powerfully picks at me like a mythical goddess. Peace.

I can't stop thinking of my previous night's dream, in which I come back to our home in Berlin to see my mother's lifeless body on the kitchen floor, a knife plunged into her chest, while Stefan laughs. Then he pulls out the bloody knife and points it at me. "It's your turn now," he says with a murderous look in his eyes. At that very moment, I stirred out of my dream, my shirt drenched in sweat. The dream seemed so real.

I swallow hard as a rush of heat runs over my body. "To hell with you, Stefan," I roar, as if I want to make sure he hears me over there in London. He needs punishment for the slaughter of so many innocent people.

"Keller." Witek's quiet voice comes from the darkness of the veranda.

Damn it. I raise my hand to silence him, and then, after looking around, I move in his direction and take a seat next to him. "What's so important that it couldn't wait till tomorrow?"

"Gestapo arrested our courier on the way back from Białystok," he says, his voice laced with concern. "With a suitcase full of pistols."

Adrenalin shoots through my system. "When?"

"About five hours ago. Jacek saw them taking her." He pauses for a moment. "At first, it looked as if they were going to let her go, but something went wrong when another guy in a black suit approached her."

"You think someone ratted?" I ask.

He shakes his head. "It was just another roundup." He sighs. "She was just in the wrong place at the wrong time."

"Does she know about me?"

"Nope," he says. "She's Anna's closest friend, though, and to me, she is like my daughter. I have known her since she was a baby." His voice is throbbing.

It's impossible to see his eyes in the darkness that surrounds us, but I sense how upset he is. Did he say Anna's closest friend? "What's her name?"

"Wanda."

A painful lump forms in my throat. "Are you sure?"

"Yes. I'm determined to do everything to help her, but the chances of freeing her are slim. She is a political prisoner, so they'll separate her from the others." He takes something out of his pocket. "I know her, Keller. She won't rat on anyone, and that means they will put her through hell." He slips a small object into my hand. "Cyanide." He clears his throat. "I need you to try to sneak it to her. She may need it."

"I can't do this," I say, clenching my hands into fists. "And I won't leave her in the hands of those animals."

He ignores me. "Most likely, they will bring her to Szucha

tomorrow morning, and on Tuesdays, Kasia sells her chocolate over there. She knows Wanda, so she should be able to see what room she is in and pass this information on to you."

"We must do more for her," I say through clenched teeth.

"I wish we could. . . " His voice cracks.

After my conversation with Witek, I enter the house and go straight to my bedroom on the second floor. My mind is racing. I'm determined to figure something out, as there is no way I will leave her in the hands of those murderers. The longer she's in their control, the less her chances of survival.

I didn't get any sleep at night, but I have a sound plan this morning. Well, more like a very courageous plan that requires a tremendous amount of luck. But I'm determined to save the girl with stormy eyes who hates me with such passion, the girl whose touch electrifies me. There is something in her that draws me like a magnet. Maybe because I like challenges, and I sense she's worth fighting for. Even if I end up paying the ultimate price, I have a deep need to try to save her.

12

Wanda

I SPEND the night in Pawiak, the Gestapo and SD prison on Dzielna Street. They dumped me in a narrow, isolated cell with an iron bed and filthy covers infested with bedbugs and fleas. After experiencing a crawling sensation on my skin, I perch in the corner of the dark and dirty cell. The air is thick; the small window is shut and nailed down. The pungent smell of urine makes me nauseous.

And yet, it isn't the darkness or the cell's poor conditions that terrify me the most; it's the thought of what will happen in the morning that paralyzes me. I want to suffocate in the airless room to avoid the terror of the Gestapo's bloody hands and possibly the hands of Alfred Kraus. I long for cyanide that offers an instant and peaceful ending. I have none of it—anxiety mounts in me. I cover my face with my trembling hands, steadying my breath.

Despite it all, I still have a naïve hope of survival. Is that a sign of stupidity? I hear Anna's words in my head: *We are at war, Wanda. You can't afford to wallow in self-pity for too long, or you won't survive. Soldiers don't cry on a battlefield; they move forward, they fight.* I close my eyes. I'm a fighter. I pray for strength during torture, but most of all, I pray for the strength to not let them break me. I've heard a lot about interrogations on Szucha and how brutal they were. At just the thought of beatings with whips and sticks, and burning, or drowning, my heart sinks.

In my mind, I picture the mistreated body of my dear friend Roman who for days was interrogated and tortured by the Gestapo. When the resistance finally freed him by attacking the lorry transporting him from Szucha to Pawiak, he was in such critical condition that he died a few days later. He didn't betray anyone, but he paid the ultimate price for his faithfulness. I want to show the same kind of strength, but is that even possible for me? No, it isn't—I'm way too weak.

Oh, Mama, I would give everything to be able to talk to you once more, to tell you how much I love you. It was a mistake to leave without talking to my mother, without hugging Kubuś.

In the morning, two guards transport me to the Gestapo headquarters on Szucha Avenue and lead me through a maze of first-floor corridors into a small room with a desk cluttered by a stack of paper files, a black telephone handset, and a lamp. The SS guard pushes me toward a chair and leaves. A small table with a typewriter adjoins the desk. They will be recording my every word. I glance at a faded picture of Hitler, who glowers at me. I scurry toward a small, curtain-less window with a view of an empty courtyard, and struggle with the handle. I fail to open it.

Soon, I hear people laughing in the corridor, so I race back to the chair. The door swings wide open, revealing Alfred Kraus chatting with a tall brunette. He pays no attention to me as he walks around the desk and settles in the large wooden chair. His female companion takes a seat at the typewriter. A broad-shouldered man in an SS uniform follows them, a whip in his hand. He is escorting a dark, curly-haired civilian in crumpled and torn clothes with black rings around his eyes and stains of dried blood on his face. The man with the whip salutes Alfred and pushes his victim through the door on my right to the adjoining room. He leaves the door open.

Alfred busies himself looking through a file on his desk while his secretary inserts paper into the typewriter. His blond hair is cut short, and he still has the same muscular physique. He shuffles the file to the side, raises his pale blue eyes, and smiles at me.

"I always admired you, Wanda," he says in German. "You were the smartest girl in our school." For a moment longer, he smiles. He stands up and walks toward me. "You had this passion for other languages, and you were pretty good at it. What was it? German, Russian, English, and Yiddish, right?"

He leans and touches my lips with his palm. "I was so damn smitten with you—my little blonde with the most beautiful eyes. I still remember our first kiss." He gazes at me for a long moment. "I planned to marry you one day, but you stood me up." His voice is quiet and tense.

I swallow hard, then pinch my lips shut to overcome the urge to spit in his face. I wish I were somewhere else, far away from this cunning man who once pretended to be the sweetest boy, and now, the man who's going to torture me once he realizes I'm not going to cooperate.

The sound of blows followed by a shriek come from the other room. It clutches at my heart.

He steps away from me. "I want to save you, Wanda." He motions to the other room with the open door. "I want to spare you this agony. If this man doesn't talk soon, they will crush his genitals, knock out his teeth, and rip out his eyes."

Curt questions and the murmur of low answers come from

the next room, followed by another crack of the whip and a man's sobs. I clutch the sides of my chair, unable to breathe.

Alfred sits back at his desk, his face serious. "Let me save you, Wanda. Tell me what location you were bringing the guns to, the names and meeting points, and most of all, tell me where your brother is," he says. "If you do just that, I promise to let you go."

I take a deep breath and meet his gaze, unblinking, "What happened to you, Alfred? What happened to that boy with a kind heart who once dreamed of building bridges? The boy who wanted nothing more than harmony and peace? The day you insulted poor Samuel, you chose to be a monster, and that day, my vision of you was crushed." I give him a pleading look. "It's not too late. You can still do the right thing."

"You were always naïve, Wanda, and I see that hasn't changed a bit." He pulls a mocking face at me.

Every nerve in my body seems to shrink.

"Give me just those few details, and I will spare you." His eyes glitter with anger.

The sound of splashing water comes from the other room, but there are no more groans or yelps of pain. The man has passed out. Hot tears well in my eyes as I avoid Alfred's gaze.

He turns to his secretary and says in a voice devoid of emotion, "Helga, walk her to the next room. It looks like she needs some encouragement."

The woman gives a satisfied smirk before standing up.

13

Finn

AFTER MEETING with Veicht at ten, I came back to my office, three doors away from his, glad to have a moment alone to think. Well, not really alone. Manfred Lange is occupying the chair on my right—the same soldier I met near Kampinos Forest. He is busy on a typewriter.

I made him my guard and secretary, with Veicht's approval, of course. Stefan's future father-in-law agreed that the extra layer of protection against the Polish *bandits* wouldn't hurt, especially when Gerda's future was at stake.

When I met Manfred for the second time, he was assigned to patrol the streets in Mokotów, my district. He ran toward me and saluted. He assumed that I was undercover the other day. I winked at him and told him to report to my office the next morning. Since then, this sixteen-year-old boy with a face full of acne has become my faithful companion, and I am determined to keep him safe. It turns out his parents died in a car accident, and he doesn't have any siblings, so he enlisted in Hitler's forces at the end of 1943. But he was in great distress when it came to performing his duties, which I had already noticed at our first encounter. I could see it in his eyes, and I knew that once he silenced his conscience, he would become one of the many who claim they are only following orders. Manfred was still struggling within himself, and I decided to help him out.

I made him believe I was Stefan until I learned more about his sensitive, artistic nature. He dreams of being a famous musician—he loves to play viola. Once he developed more trust in me, I brought him on board with my mission. It turns out he is a perfect fit and eager to fight for the right thing. He doesn't speak Polish, but still, he is instrumental as my messenger with the resistance. That works well, as it's an excellent help to Jacek, who is in far more danger than a uniformed Manfred.

Everything in Stefan's office is in perfect order—things lined up on my desk, files locked away in the black iron cabinet. Stefan left a terrible mess, making me wonder how anyone could function under such conditions.

"Did you get the answer?" I ask in a quiet voice.

He nods and fishes out a small paper ball from his pocket.

I untangle it and read, *Approved.* I like how simple Witek has always been. But mostly, we are good to go. At the thought of my insane plan, a surge of adrenalin shoots through my veins. I need to get distracted.

"Elkstein, the commander of Arbeitsamt, was killed on Skaryszewska Street, along with two Poles." For the next hour, I dictate the report to Manfred. When I finish, my watch shows a quarter after eleven. "Manfred, Obersturmbannführer Veicht is expecting the report by this afternoon. Make sure to apply the changes as I just told you."

"Yes, sir."

Hearing a rapid door knock, my body tenses. "Come in," I say.

An attractive blonde in her early twenties puts her head in the door. "*Guten Tag.* Chocolate?" she asks in accented German.

She's wearing a charcoal suit with a logo of "E. Wedel" on her left breast pocket. I learned from Witek that this young woman named Kasia works at the Polish confectionery and is also a member of the resistance. Chocolate is hard to come by, even for Germans, so she is allowed to distribute it in this building. Thanks to her eavesdropping, she is able to supply the underground with important information—such as room numbers and private addresses of the Gestapo officers—including that of my brother.

"Yes, please, come in. What can you recommend today?" I smile at her, glancing at a brown wooden box she's holding.

"Helga in room 109 likes the chocolate-covered candy," she says with a meaningful look on her pretty face. "The others are too busy with a prisoner."

A lighthearted feeling spreads through me. I tell Manfred, whose cheeks flame with color as he gazes at Kasia, to choose whatever he likes while I phone Gerda. I make plans with her to meet at Café Anna at one o'clock. Wanda is in room 109. That means that bastard Alfred Kraus is interrogating her. It makes it all the harder, as the man is a cruel son of a bitch. But he has a crush on Gerda, and I plan to take advantage of it.

After Kasia leaves, I point to the chair holding a set of clothes Zuzanna wrapped last night in brown paper—the same way most laundromats in Warsaw do. "Bring that to me in fifteen minutes in room 109 and tell me I forgot the laundry," I say, my eyes fixed on Manfred.

"Yes, sir." The color leaves his face. "Is that Kraus's office?"

"Yup." I pat his arm. "We'll be fine; we just have to stick to our plan. Are you okay?"

"Yes, sir," he says, his face twisted into a scowl. "I just hate that monster."

* * *

I find Kraus at his desk in a cheerful mood, smoking a cigarette and flirting with his secretary, who is eating chocolate. The door to the interrogation room is wide open, so on my way toward Kraus, I catch a glimpse of Wanda straddled on the wooden chair, her face stained with blood. A large man with a hide whip in his hand stands beside her, asking her something.

I force my mouth into a smile. "I'm jealous. I see you are having a lot of fun here while I'm bored to death at my office." Kraus and my brother had a casual manner, as they spent a lot of time drinking together.

Kraus looks up and smiles at me through cigarette smoke. "Look who's here. I thought you'd forgotten all about me." He raises an eyebrow. "I was under the impression you didn't like me anymore, my friend."

Why is he saying that? I guess he is disappointed I don't go drinking and visiting brothels with him as Stefan did. "Come on, you know you are my favorite," I say while we shake hands. "Just so busy lately. And Fräulein Veicht likes me to herself very much, too." I wink at him.

He breaks into a laugh. "I don't blame you. I wouldn't say no to our beautiful Fräulein, either. How is she?"

"She is fine, thank you. I'm meeting with her for lunch at Café Anna at one, and I promised to bring you along so that we can catch up. Are you up to it?" At the sound of whip blows and Wanda's sobs, my heart plummets into the pit of my stomach.

His eyes light up. "Oh yes, most certainly. We all could use a break here." He motions to the interrogation room. "We have another stubborn bitch. I used to date that slut, so I tried to get the information from her by sweet-talking, but she is too stubborn. No matter. If the whip doesn't make her talk, we'll knock her teeth out," he says.

"Relax, Alfred. It's easy to make them talk. I guess your people don't do their job right." I shoot him a mocking smile.

More whip cracks, more sobs. My heart breaks, but my mind remains sharp.

He frowns. "I know her, Stefan. She would rather die than talk, so that's her fate."

"What is the use of that? The whole purpose is to get the important information out of them so we can use it against those Polish bastards." I gesture toward the other room. "You need someone better for this job."

"There is no one better than Klaus."

"I bet I can make her talk."

He grins. "I have to admit you were very good at it. Why did you stop helping us?"

"I told you, no time. But I must admit, I miss my whip." I force a sardonic laugh. "Tell you what, let me have some fun while you go ahead and meet with Gerda. Tell her I'll be there soon. I'll make that whore of yours talk, but on the condition that you pay for my drinks today."

There is a knock at the door. Manfred politely informs me about my forgotten laundry.

I ignore him and meet Kraus's gaze. "Deal?"

He nods. "Deal. Do you need my secretary?"

"Nope. She can take her lunch break. Send that useless jerk out, too," I say, motioning toward the interrogation room. "I have a better man for the job." I point to Manfred, who stands with his chest out and a serious expression spoiled only by the scratched acne that is now bleeding.

Kraus is eager to get on his way to meet Gerda. He sends his secretary and the butcher man for a break. "When you are done having fun, send her to the trams. I will continue with her when I get back," he says.

Trams. I hate those basement cells equipped with wooden benches where prisoners await interrogation.

The moment they depart, we race to Wanda, as we only have an hour before Kraus's secretary returns. She lies motionless on the floor, her pale face covered with blood. Her battered hands indicate that she tried to protect her head. Rage envelops me. At the same time, I know they've only just started with her, so the only visible damage is to her head and hands.

As adrenalin shoots through my veins, my mind is more sober than ever. I spot the bucket of water they use to awaken victims, and I splash some of it onto Wanda's face. When she opens her eyes, I send Manfred to Kraus's office to look out for any visitors.

I help her to sit upright. Her head flinches back when she touches her face with her trembling hand. Her gaze holds a flash of shock. "No, no, no, I don't know anything." She then squeezes her eyes shut, as if she's awaiting another blow.

"Listen to me, Wanda." I pause and wait until she opens her eyes. "I want to take you out of here, but I need your help, sweetie. Can you help me?"

"I... I don't understand."

"Anna sent me to save you." The lie comes to me quickly. I'm confident it's the best way to convince her to trust me, or at least cooperate.

"Anna sent you?" she asks.

"Yes. I'm going to dress you in clean clothes, and we will walk out of this building together. You must use all your strength to walk by my side." I don't wait for her response. I dip my handkerchief in the bucket of leftover water and clean the streams of blood from her face and neck. When she winces in pain, I encourage her to scream. In this building, it is just a sign of a well-done job. She cooperates. I dress her in an elegant, long-sleeved black dress, stockings, black slippers, black leather gloves, and a large hat with a net covering her face and neck. By the time I finish, we still have twenty minutes before Helga's return, unless she decides to come back early. I wrap her old clothes and my wet handkerchief in the brown paper and spill the bloody water to the floor.

I instruct Manfred to take a walk and check the corridors. It's peak lunch hour, but we still need to encounter as few people as possible on our way.

He comes back ten minutes later. "The hall is empty now."

"Now, beautiful, hide your face in the crook of my arm and try to walk with my support. Don't hesitate to sob. You have to stay in that position while we walk to my car," I say. "At no time lift your head, sweetie." I tell Manfred to pick up the package with Wanda's old clothes and to hold her other arm. We walk through a maze of first-floor corridors without meeting anyone until one guard stops us near the front entrance.

"Hauptsturmführer Keller. Do you need help?" he asks, surveying Wanda between Manfred and I.

"No, I have it under control. The wife of my friend killed by those Polish bandits visited me, and she just had a nervous breakdown."

He narrows his eyes. "I've been here since the early morning, and I haven't seen this lady coming in. Frau, can I see your face?"

I raise my voice. "Are you telling me you've been fooling around instead of watching the place? If you missed this lady, you most certainly missed someone else, too. Should I ask Obersturmbannführer Veicht to assign you to a less important task?"

His face reflects confusion at first, but then a sign of hesitation flashes over it. "I apologize, sir. I did step away for a minute or two. Please forgive me for my error." He salutes.

"Fine. Make sure to do your job right."

"Yes, sir."

Once we are outside, Manfred runs to get my car. Wanda is losing her strength, so I'm thankful we can stand in place while I support her limp body. Soon enough, we're driving away in the direction of the Mokotów district.

We leave Wanda in the care of Zuzanna. Then we drive to the café, where I tell Anna that Kraus can't leave the place until morning. She is to put a sleeping powder in his drink and lure him upstairs so he sleeps throughout the rest of the day and night.

I take Kraus aside and explain that I couldn't stop myself from beating the girl to death. "Manfred dumped her body at a disposal site. And no worries, my friend, I will take care of the paperwork."

"I told you she was a stubborn bitch. But I wish you'd held your horses and kept her alive for us."

"You're right, but the pleasure I took from it makes it worth it. Your drinks are on me."

An hour later, Kraus accepts Anna's invitation to go upstairs. I drive Gerda back home, return to my office, and make the official report on Wanda's *death*.

The whole time I was acting the part of my brother, who enjoyed torturing innocent people. Stefan's unflinching cruelty scares the hell out of me. How is it possible that someone who shares my genes could be such a monster?

A couple of days later, Kraus runs out of luck when he is shot dead by a trespasser outside his villa in Żoliborz.

14

Wanda

Two weeks later, Finn's villa in Mokotów

I stand beside a white-tiled stove, stirring pickle soup in a large, iron pot. Mrs. Zuzanna Kowalska started it before she went shopping, and now the steamy kitchen air is filled with the aroma of dill pickles.

For the first week, I mainly stayed in bed, letting my body heal. When I realized that the man who saved me left early in the morning and was gone late into the night, I started moving around. Mrs. Kowalska, a short, cramped woman in her mid-seventies with gray hair and a soft, wrinkled face, has been so kind to relay to me the man's message that to the Gestapo, I'm dead. He advised me against returning to my home since it's now monitored for signs of my brother, as they suspect I was working with him.

I like to spend time with Mrs. Kowalska, who never stops talking, and with her grandchildren, who have been living in the house for the last two months. Mrs. Kowalska's son and daughter-in-law, who worked for the resistance, were arrested and brought to Pawiak. They both died as the result of torture at Szucha Avenue. All three children survived because they were at the underground school at the time of the arrest.

It shocks me that the man tolerates the children here; Mrs. Kowalska said he even brings food and money. Even though he risked his life to save me from that hell at Szucha, I can't erase from my mind the night he killed my father. Why is he helping me now?

I sense someone standing at the kitchen door behind me. It's not Mrs. Kowalska, as she has gone shopping. It must be him.

"Good morning." His voice comes from a distance.

I force my mouth into a smile. "Good morning. Would you like anything to eat? I'm not a good cook, but I can put together something simple."

"Just a black coffee will do, and maybe a piece of that delicious sawdust bread," he says, a teasing smile crossing his face.

His attempt to lighten the air between us makes me even more uncomfortable. I don't know what to say or do anymore. The same man who killed my father also saved my life, and it wasn't guilt that made him do it. I'm sure of that.

"We also have the white bread you brought the other day," I say to cut the silence between us.

"Save that for the children." His smiling eyes search my face.

I hand his coffee and bread over, and I'm about to walk out of the kitchen when he takes my arm. "Can you keep me company? I hate eating alone."

I hesitate but sit on the other side of the small table. I move aside a vase with cut sunflowers from Mrs. Kowalska's garden. "I never thanked you for saving my life," I say, glancing at him.

He sips his coffee. "I'm glad my plan worked." His gray eyes brighten. He looks tired, with dark shadows under his eyes, but still, he appears immaculate in his gray uniform and with his dark blond hair combed back. I still detect the clean, masculine scent of his aftershave, and there is just a hint of woodsy cologne in the air.

I need to stop it, and right now. I can't possibly view him as a human. He's a Nazi; even though he saved my life, he killed Tata and many others. Who knows what his intentions are, anyway? I should run away at the first chance.

"Are you okay?" he asks, watching me.

I can't hold back any longer. "Do you want the honest answer, or you would rather stick with politeness?"

"The honest one," he says, his voice quiet.

"I keep wondering what's the real purpose of you saving me. So you can have more fun later?"

He draws his eyebrows together in a frown. "What do you mean?"

"You know what I mean," I say, unable to remove the bitter note from my voice.

"No, I don't, so please tell me." He speaks in a somewhat weary tone.

"Murderers don't suddenly change into good Samaritans overnight, you know." Oh, God, why did I say that? I just gave him a reason to kill me.

He rubs the back of his neck. "The fact I wear this uniform doesn't make me a murderer."

Does he really think it doesn't? I can't take his games anymore. "Have you forgotten the night you came to my home and killed my father?" With a pounding in my ears, I lose control of myself.

He gives me a blank look. "I never came to your home." There is no anger, only finality in his voice.

"Do you still have my sunflower painting you stole that night?"

The moment I attempt to walk away, he surges to his feet and presses me to the wall, his face inches from mine. "I'm not sure what you are talking about, but I do have an identical twin brother. He is in custody in London right now, and I'm pretending to be him. I swear, I didn't kill your father, and I never broke into your home." He maintains his grip on me. "What I just told you must be kept a secret. Only a few people know it." He releases me. "My name is Finn, not Stefan. And I'm truly sorry to hear about your father."

When he walks away, I can't move. My arms ache from his touch. I listen to the rumbling of his car engine outside, and then there is silence. He is gone. Is he telling the truth, or is this another game? He did introduce himself as Finn when I bumped into him in the Old Town. And then, as Stefan when he came to our house. Have I met two different men within a day, thinking they were one? Have I tried to kill the innocent man, thinking he was Tata's murderer? I don't know what to think anymore.

"It's going to be a hot day," Mrs. Kowalska says as she enters the kitchen carrying a wooden basket filled with groceries. "I saw Stefan leaving. First time in weeks he slept longer." She sighs. "I feel bad for him."

I want to yell at her to stop sympathizing with the Nazi. Or is she one of the people who knows his real identity? "How long has he been living in your house?"

"Since January of 1943. Why do you ask?"

"Just out of curiosity. He seems to have a good heart, despite his bloody uniform," I say, helping her unpack the groceries.

"He does. And let me assure you that his uniform carried blood on it only after he saved you."

I nod, not willing to argue with her. Maybe she is right after all, and perhaps he is telling the truth. "I promised Tosia I would read more of that book to her."

"That's fine, sweetheart. You can go get them now," she says, a smile lighting up her soft face. "We'll eat at one o'clock."

Tosia is twelve, Basia is seven, and Alek is five. Every day from ten in the morning until two in the afternoon, they gather in the large family room on the house's first floor. The rest of the time they spend upstairs, in the bedroom down the hall. While they are in the family room, the window curtains are drawn tight, and we are alerted to any noises from outside. Once in a while, unexpected visitors come looking for Stefan, most often his fiancée and her father. They usually visit in the late afternoon. But one never knows as the Gestapo sneak around without warning.

Once downstairs, Tosia perches on the sofa in the large family room with a book in her hand. She is deep into *Anne of Green Gables* by L. M. Montgomery, and she waits for me to read it to her. The book is in English, so I have been translating it into Polish for her. I found it in one of the rooms upstairs and encouraged the shy, quiet girl to read it with me. Mrs. Kowalska's daughter, Beata, who is in her forties, lives in Canada, and since the war started, she hasn't been able to visit. Mrs. Kowalska keeps talking about her other two granddaughters, whom she misses so much. One of them left the book.

There are many other things left behind from the summer of 1939, the last year they visited. I'm thankful for the clothes I have been borrowing from her daughter. I'm her height and build, so those outfits look like they were made especially for me. The only issue is that she clearly prefers light-colored fabrics, and I'm still in mourning after Tata. I know my father would understand.

I'm not good with children, so from the very beginning, I have been unsure how to approach them. These kids have been separated from their parents, unaware of their deaths. I'm not sure about Tosia, though—her eyes have a sad expression that brings sorrow to my heart. Maybe she suspects the truth.

Basia helps Mrs. Kowalska in the kitchen. She adores her grandma to the point she follows her everywhere. Alek plays with a wooden train set on the soft divan, making chugging sounds.

Halfway through the first page of Tosia's book, I pause at a sudden knock on a door.

"It must be your friend Anna," Mrs. Kowalska says from the kitchen. Then she's walking toward us, wiping her hands on her apron. "Stefan did ask me to tell you she was going to visit you this morning, but it slipped my mind."

At the mention of Anna, joy wells up in my heart. "Let me go with the children upstairs until we know for sure it's her," I say.

She nods.

In no time, we are upstairs waiting in the children's bedroom to be called back by Mrs. Kowalska. Meanwhile, I can't help but wonder if Anna has had an affair with Stefan. Or Finn? I don't know anymore. Are they in love? If he is Finn, in truth, then I am okay with it. But if he's lying to me, and he is Stefan, that changes everything. Maybe the resistance needs information and asked her to get involved with him. After all, if not for him, I would be dead by now.

"Wanda, you can come out," Anna's soothing voice comes from the hall.

* * *

"I wanted to come earlier, but Keller asked me to wait a couple of weeks, just to be safe," Anna says fifteen minutes later. She glances toward the kitchen, where all three children are helping Mrs. Kowalska prepare rabbit pâté. We sit at a dining table and sip an ersatz coffee. Anna leans across the table and covers my hand with hers. "I have been worrying about you, but I see Keller has been taking good care of you."

"He has," I say, "but why is he doing this?" I focus on her pale blue eyes. "What's his real intention?"

She moves her hand away and tilts her head back. "You have nothing to worry about. There is not much I can tell you, it's safer that way, but I assure you his intentions are good. You can trust him as much as you trust me."

I rub my chin. Maybe he did tell me the truth after all, and his brother is the one who killed Tata. I still find it hard to believe it, though. "Are you... I mean, is he... ?" My face and ears feel hot. "Are you having an affair with him?"

A laugh breaks through her crimson-red lips that match her elegant suit. "Of course not. He's not even my type. The only thing I can tell you is that we work together on the mission of defeating Hitler. He is crucial for the resistance efforts." She winks at me. "And there is only one man on this earth that I'm interested in." She sighs. "You know him very well."

I feel an unexpected release of tension. Is she talking about my brother? They never dated, but I know Mateusz is in love with her. When I confronted him about it, he replied that he wasn't worthy of her because she needs an artistic man who can understand her better, and not just an ordinary doctor. So there is only friendship between them.

"And who is that lucky man?" I ask.

A glimmer of laughter comes into her eyes. "The most daring and funniest man in the world. He also happens to be your brother," she says. "The man I'm worried sick for every day."

"He's fine, Anna." I beam at her. "He's hiding in the woods with the other partisans near my family's estate."

She gasps. "How do you know?"

"I met him on the way back home from Tosaki. Witek told him to disappear after that German commander was killed."

"I can't believe Witek hid it from us," she says with annoyance.

"He asked about you," I say.

A smile ignites her face. "How's he doing?"

* * *

Two hours later, Anna is gone and we're sitting at the dining table. Mrs. Kowalska says a short prayer, and we eat the pickle soup. Tosia settles next to Alek, reminding him to eat every time he reaches for a little wooden train on his lap. But then, we hear rumblings of a car engine outside. As adrenalin rushes through me, I leap to my feet and spring to the window. "It's just Finn," I say, turning to look at Mrs. Kowalska.

She contemplates for a short moment. "Thank the Lord, it's only *Stefan*," she says, glancing at me as she heads toward the kitchen to reappear with another place setting.

"You are just in time to have this delicious soup Wanda made." She smiles at Finn when he enters the room a minute later.

"Can't wait," he says, looking at the children, who, to my surprise, charge toward him. "Uncle, look, I have a train." Little Alek smiles when Finn picks him up to give him an airplane ride, the boy squealing with delight.

"Now my turn, please, Uncle." Basia tugs on his sleeve. He lowers Alek down and picks her up. Tosia doesn't move from the chair; she just looks at Finn with a gentle smile that almost reaches her eyes. Those kids never respond that way to me. He is so good with them.

When we finally resume our seats, the children's faces are red and cheerful.

"This soup looks very tempting," Finn says, glancing at me.

Heat rises to my cheeks. "Thank you," I say, averting my eyes. All this about him is so new. After the conversation with Anna, it's clear to me he's a good guy. How is it possible that identical twins are so different, one a Nazi killer, while the other helps the resistance?

"I couldn't make it better myself," Mrs. Kowalska says.

"Uncle, I helped *Babcia* (Grandma) make rabbit *pasztet*," Basia says.

He grins at her. "You are my favorite cook, Princess." Then he looks at Tosia. "What have you been up to?"

"She stayed on the sofa all day." Basia's facial expression shows pity. "I think she was reading."

"Not your business, you nosy brat." Tosia glares at her sister.

"What have you been reading?" Finn asks.

"*Anne of Green Gables*. It's in English, but Miss Wanda reads it to me in Polish." Her voice is full of excitement.

"Is it about a little girl with red hair?"

"Yes." Her eyes light up.

He looks at me and leans forward. "I take it your English is good?"

"I guess I can get by." I smile, and something heavy releases its pressure off my heart.

15

Finn

I EXCUSE MYSELF TO GERDA, pretending to have a bad headache. It's near nine when I enter the quiet villa and find Zuzanna at the small kitchen table, peeling onions.

"Do you need some help, Zuzanna?" I ask, unable to suppress a smile. From the beginning, she told me to call her by name as she claims it makes her feel younger.

She looks at me through her tearing, red eyes. "Oh, yes, I could use another pair of hands."

I grab a small knife and sit across from her. "I guess we'll have onion soup tomorrow?"

"I got some *boczek*, bacon, and was planning to fry it with onion."

I nod. "How did you manage to have everyone asleep on the dot?"

"Don't let them fool you." She bursts into a brief laugh. "Those rascals won't close their eyes until they get at least three stories out of poor Wanda."

"She tells them stories?" I peel the last onion and watch Zuzanna cut the first one into long strips. Then I copy her.

"Yes, and she seems to have the patience for it. You won't believe me if I tell you that she thinks she's not good with kids."

"Really?" The damn onion finally gets to me, making my vision hazy.

"She is so gentle with Tosia." She sighs. "It breaks my heart just to look at my little girl, so I'm glad Wanda found a way to reach her."

"Tosia suspects the truth. I can see it in her eyes." After cutting one onion while Zuzanna manages to slice six of them, I go to the small sink and wash the tears off my face. "Goddammit, onion."

She laughs with delight. "Well, thanks for your help, sweetheart. Do you want me to make you supper?"

"I ate with Gerda." I kiss her forehead. She reminds me of my grandma, who passed away five years ago, leaving my grandpa heartbroken.

She rolls her eyeballs. "Be careful with that snake of a woman," she says.

I sigh. "I know. Hopefully, she'll leave for Berlin soon. For now, though, I must keep her contained."

"I pray for your strength and wisdom. I notice the way you look at Wanda."

I gaze out the window, feeling the heat rise to my cheeks.

"She has a tender spot in your heart, my boy. And let me tell you that she seems to blush every time you speak or look at her, too."

I grimace at the memory of a few days earlier. "You should have seen the way she glared at me when she thought I was Stefan."

"It's good you told her the truth."

I nod. "Somehow, I trust her more than myself."

"I feel bad for you young people. Love doesn't agree with

war," she says, a meaningful look in her eyes. "Were you ever in love before?"

"No, and who knows if I ever will be."

"My late husband said that fighting true feelings is the silliest thing a man can do." Her voice softens. "Especially if tomorrow is not guaranteed."

*   *   *

Zuzanna's last words play in my mind while I shower and change into a clean, white cotton t-shirt and black trousers. No, tomorrow isn't guaranteed. What would happen if fate gave me a chance to know Wanda in ordinary times? I dated so many women back home, but none of them excited me the way she has since my first glance at her.

I walk down the hall to the last door on the right—the kids' room. It's quiet, so I assume they are already asleep; still, I want to check on them. All three are fast asleep on the double bed while Wanda sits next to them in the rocking chair. She is awake, watching them with pure admiration. At the same time, there is a hint of pain in her eyes. The bruises on her face and hands have almost faded away. She's wearing a yellow, short-sleeved shirt that makes an exciting combination with her sapphire eyes and golden-walnut hair coiled into a topknot. It strikes me that this is the first time I've seen her wearing light colors. She is the epitome of fragile beauty, conflicting with the inner strength rooted within her. My fingers ache to trace her delicate features.

When she looks at me, there is a hint of sorrow in her eyes. She slips from the room without another glance at me. I turn off the light and follow her, overpowered by the strange, gnawing need for her warmth and affection. The foreign feeling of longing grows in me to the point where it hurts.

"Good night," she says, looking up at me, her voice gentle. She's no more than five feet tall, but at that moment, she holds absolute power, even though she doesn't realize it. She turns away.

"Wait." I finally manage to get a word out. "Would you like to join me for a drink?" My voice sounds pathetic, even to me. I dated more women in a month than some men in a lifetime, so why am I feeling like a novice?

When she turns back, a shy smile appears on her lips. "Only if it's something other than vodka."

I grin. "Do you like red wine?"

Her mouth twists into a knowing smile. "Well, Mrs. Kowalska did say to try her homemade wine."

"Right," I say, trying to keep my voice neutral. One day I will have her taste the finest wine in the world. One day my entire world will be hers. I chase my absurd thoughts away. "There is a balcony off my bedroom with a view of the garden. Would you like to sit there?"

"Sure."

"Great. Let me grab the famous wine."

* * *

We stare at the sky full of stars and drink Zuzanna's homemade wine that is way too sweet, in my opinion, but I sense that Wanda's enjoying it. The silence between us isn't uncomfortable; it feels good. One thing I've noticed about her is her inability to make small talk. She goes straight to the point with matters, and I know the same thing will happen tonight.

"I thought you were like Jekyll and Hyde."

I choke on my wine, and she pats my back. "Hopefully, now I'm only Dr. Jekyll."

"Are you?" Her eyes rise to meet mine, transfixing me.

I want to tell her at least some things about me, even though it's safer for her when she doesn't know much. "I lived with my parents and my twin brother, Stefan, in Germany until I was fifteen." In short, I tell her the rest of my story.

"Were you close to your brother growing up?"

"I thought I was, but when I think about it now, we were always fighting. I didn't take it seriously until I found him trying to kill our mother with a kitchen knife when we were ten. At first, I thought he was just pretending, but then I saw this anger in his eyes that scared the hell out of me. And the only reason he wanted to murder her was that she refused to buy him a new toy. Our mother kept sending him for treatment, but he always found a way to wind up in trouble.

"When I think about my brother, I think about that one summer day when we were fourteen and visited my Aunt Helga, who lives about forty kilometers from Berlin. She had a little kitten that she adored.

"One day, my aunt sent me to summon Stefan for supper. I found him in the nearby woods watching the little kitten going up in flames. I'll never forget the satisfied look on Stefan's face. I was too late to save the kitten, but I've felt no connection with my brother since that day. I stopped trying to look for good things in him because there weren't any. A year later, I emigrated with my mother to America and hadn't seen him until I came for my mission here. And this time, it isn't just about a kitten; it's about killing innocent people. He is one cruel son of a bitch."

"I'm so sorry." There is a faint catch in her voice.

"I'm the one who should apologize for my brother." Our eyes meet and I take in her sorrow, hating my brother more than ever. "What about you?" I whisper with a heavy heart. "I understand if it's too hard to talk about what happened to your father."

"No." She takes a deep breath. "I would like to tell you about it."

As she describes her ordeal, a lump rises in my throat. "I'm so sorry," I whisper when she falls silent.

She buries her face in her hands.

I want to wrap her in my arms and soothe her with tender words, but I'm frozen in place. I'm sure she doesn't want me to touch her.

She straightens and wipes her tears. "Please, forgive me. It must be hard on you too, to know that your brother—" She reaches out to touch my arm, sending a shiver of emotion through my body. "Please don't apologize for him. You are not him. It just makes me wonder how different you both are. And from what you are saying, your mother is a good woman."

"She truly is. It's my father who brought evil to our family. I always wondered what made her fall in love with him. Even in my early memories, he was detached from us, busy supporting the Nazi Party. I have only a few good memories of him from when I was little.

"According to my mom, he wasn't always like that. At the beginning of their relationship, my mother was his entire world. He changed when we were about seven, and he began working closely with Hitler. There were no more vacations together. He was always out, neglecting my brother and me, and when he was home, he drank and took out his frustrations on my mother. She often ended up with black eyes when he drank too much. I hated him and swore to kill him one day.

"He was a psychopath, always blaming my mother for something. My brother and I had to listen to his long speeches about our future as the chosen ones, about his hatred, particularly of Poles and Jews. He treated our Polish nanny with contempt. Maybe he's the reason for my brother's evil." I sigh. "But that's enough about my family."

Over the following weeks it becomes our habit to meet on the balcony once everyone is asleep. I learn a lot about her, and she learns a lot about me. I know her favorite color, book, and song, but still, I don't know if she feels the same about me as I do about her. She acts like we are good friends now, while I have to contain the desperate need to caress her body. I wish she could hear the chaotic thumping of my heart every time she comes near me.

One night she doesn't show up. I wait for nearly an hour before the thought that she's bored with me enters my mind. Heat flushes through my body as I walk to her door and knock, but she doesn't answer. A minute later, though, she emerges from the children's sleeping room; she seems startled.

"I'm sorry I didn't join you today, but Tosia couldn't fall asleep, and I didn't want to leave her alone with her anxiety."

I feel relief sweeping over me. "I understand. Go to bed— you look tired."

Instead of walking away, she touches my tense jaw with her hand. "I can sense you are still upset."

A desire runs through my veins, exciting every fiber in my miserable body. Oh, God, how I want her. I pull her close to me and cover her soft lips with my mouth. She responds by putting her hand in my hair as our kiss turns steamy and powerful. Her mouth tastes like salty air on a crisp morning. I put my hand under her pajama shirt and trace her bare skin. It feels absolute; she is my absolute.

When I lift my mouth, she backs off, her cheeks flushed. "Good night, Finn."

"Good night, beauty." When she's gone, I can't bring myself to walk away, so I remain there staring at her door. The sweet scent of her body still lingers in my nostrils; the softness of her skin still loiters on my hands. She's either playing with me, or she doesn't want me, not yet.

16

Wanda

I WAKE up to birds chirping outside, and I can't help but smile at the memory of Finn's kiss last night. His touch felt so good. I spent most of the night thinking of him and the way he looked at me like he didn't want to let me go.

I know it's still very early, probably no more than six, but I can't wait to see him again. He has this habit of an early coffee. I wash my face in the bathroom sink and put on an ocean-blue, short-sleeved dress. I spend a good fifteen minutes pinning my hair up—something totally foreign to me, as it usually takes me no more than a minute.

I must stop this. I don't need to impress him with my looks. We are just friends, and it should stay that way. Not so long ago, I thought he was Tata's murderer. He is not, but his brother is. And here I am trying to seduce him. I unpin my hair and let it loose. It's not important how I look. There are more critical things to worry about.

The strong aroma of ersatz coffee fills the kitchen air. He sits at the table, his head down.

"Good morning," I say and smile. In my heart, I'm thrilled

to see him.

He gives me a startled look, but he doesn't return my smile. "Good morning." His voice is soft and almost sad.

"Are you all right?" I ask with genuine concern. "Are you ill?"

"No, not all." His gentle smile chases my worries away. "I just have a tough day ahead, and I'm trying to plan things."

"I won't bother you then. We can talk later." I step back to turn around, but he takes my hand.

"Please stay. I have been up all night planning, so I can use a break and enjoy your company." His voice and eyes ache with pleading.

For the next half hour, we chat about ordinary things. When he stands up to leave, our eyes meet, and the endless longing in his arouses warmth inside me. I desperately want him to kiss me again, to feel his lips on mine, but he turns away and leaves.

I get myself busy with children through the rest of the day and manage to not think about him at all. However, when he is not back for supper and not even for the night, worries keep me awake.

"Finn didn't get back last night," I say in the morning to Mrs. Kowalska, who just entered the kitchen with a wicker basket in her hand.

"I noticed that." I help her put away a loaf of black bread, two tiny portions of beetroot-colored marmalade, and lard. That would have to last us a whole week if not for Finn's help and Mrs. Kowalska's savviness. I'm surprised she was able to get so much food after only one outing. It's ridiculous how little produce we are allowed to purchase with the ration cards.

She sighs. "I take it he spent the night with that evil woman." There is a trace of disapproval in her voice.

I drop an empty basket onto the floor. She thinks Finn spent the night with Gerda. That's ridiculous. Then the truth about him hits me. He couldn't get into my bed, so he settled for Gerda's.

"Are you okay, sweetie?" she asks with concern. "You look pale."

"I have a migraine today." I lie, wanting to cover my embarrassing reaction to the news about Finn.

"Go take some rest. I will tell the children not to be too loud."

I need to compose myself. "I'm fine. I promised Tosia to read some more of her book." I touch her arm. "Your beautiful grandchildren are the best cure for any illness."

The day goes by fast. I spend time with the kids and then dust and scrub the floors because I don't know how to deal with my anger. I'm pathetic to care what Finn does in his free time. It's his business, not mine, but I'm upset with myself for this heavy feeling in my chest.

He finally shows up in time for supper. Mrs. Kowalska serves sour milk with potatoes, Finn's favorite dish.

"Thank you for making such a delicious supper, ladies." He smiles at Mrs. Kowalska and glances at me. I haven't been paying him much attention after greeting him coolly.

"I made it," Basia says with pride. "It didn't take long since the milk was already a little sour."

"What an excellent cook you are, sweetie. It tastes amazing and so refreshing." He eats another spoonful of it, and something in me snaps. I know I'm about to do something ridiculous, but I don't care. I jerk the bowl away from him, pour the white liquid over his styled hair, and laugh. "I think that might be even more refreshing."

He makes no move, and since his face is now covered with sour milk, I can't see his expression. But I'm feeling much better, and I don't regret my action a bit.

"Wanda," Mrs. Kowalska says in a stunned voice.

"Whatever came over you?" The children stare with gaping mouths.

I say nothing. I walk away, lock the bedroom door, and collapse onto the bed. Soon the initial thrill of my audacity wears off, and I feel ashamed of myself and dissolve into weeping.

Why did I have to react so impetuously, like a silly child? This man has done nothing to me besides save my life and be kind, and I just treated him like an enemy. I have to apologize, but I need more time to gather my strength. I'm afraid to look into his eyes, and worse, I'm worried he will ask why I did it. I will have to fabricate a lie. I can't tell him the truth because he will think I'm jealous and pity me.

Several painful hours pass before I hear a tentative knock on the door. I bolt upright. The knock comes again, but I can't bring myself to answer.

"Wanda." His quiet voice makes me bury my face in my hands. "Please open the door."

I ignore him, hoping he will think I'm asleep and leave, but he doesn't relent.

"If you don't open within two minutes, I will break the door down," he says. "And I don't think Zuzanna will like it."

I don't doubt he will, so I slip toward the door. When I open it, I avoid his eyes by staring at his broad chest covered with a crisp white T-shirt. The scent of chamomile soap tingles my nostrils. He smells so good. "I'm sorry for what I did," I say without meeting his gaze. "It was so childish of me."

"Please let me in." His voice is soft but insistent. "We need to talk."

I take my hand off the doorknob and gesture for him to come in. The room is tiny, so the bed takes up almost the entire space. I take a seat on the edge of the bed, and so does he.

"I'm sorry I missed our gathering at the balcony last night.

Witek wanted me to be a part of a meeting, and by the time we were done, it was so late that I slept at his flat," he says, taking my hand in his.

I feel an unexpected rush of relief. "You don't need to explain yourself to me." He thinks I'm jealous. That's so embarrassing, especially as it's true. "That's not why I dumped the milk on you. I just had this rash moment when you reminded me of Stefan," I lie, not knowing what else to say.

There is a long silence between us that slices through my heart. When I master enough courage to look at him, I see sadness and resignation in his face.

"I can't help that we look alike," he whispers, and that's when something breaks in me.

"I'm so sorry I just lied to you. You don't remind me of him at all. I just thought that you spent the night with Gerda, and...."

He kneels in front of me and takes my hands. "I would never do that. You are the only one I want to be with."

His boldness brings heat to my face. "We can't do this," I whisper.

"Only if you want it as much I do. Or I will leave now, and tomorrow we will start over." He gives me his most charming smile, and my heart melts.

"Stay," I say, surprising myself.

"What did you just say?" He grins. "You want me to leave now?"

I laugh and smack him playfully in the chest. "I said I want you to stay."

"Then tell me you will never stop trusting me." He has an earnest look on his face. "You have made my heart so vulnerable." His fingers caress my cheek.

"I will never stop trusting you," I say as my tears start to flow.

17

Gerda

1 August 1944

Dear Mutti,

It's been nearly four months since my last letter and no response from you. But since we are at war, your letter must have been lost on its way. If I didn't know you any better, I would think you are upset with me, but that's not the case because I know how much you love me. And after all, I saved you from sheltering those parasites. I still don't understand why you let them hide in our home. They must have somehow brainwashed you to commit that awful crime. Yes, Mutti, for sheltering undesirables in Warsaw, you would have been given the death penalty. Papa said Ravensbrück would put you on the right track so that you can come back to us. I believe him, but it makes me worry to even think about you when I realize how far you are from us. I miss you so much, and there is not a day when I don't think about you.

Papa told me to pack, as I will be leaving for Berlin in five days. He thinks it's very unsafe for me in Warsaw, and it is supposed to get even worse as those Polish bandits are preparing something big. Well, I have a feeling he is right. Just looking at those dirty streets gives me nausea, and it seems like those filthy animals have changed the way they look at us. It's like they are less afraid of the Führer or they are awaiting something. Papa got drunk again last night, and he kept telling me that the Soviets are coming for us. It was just drunk blubber, but still, I'll be glad to leave in a few days.

Oh, Mutti, you can't even imagine how broken my heart is right now. My Stefan betrayed me.

Yesterday, I planned to surprise him by stopping by his office to take him for lunch, but his secretary informed me that he had left. He didn't say where, but I decided to check out his villa. His black Mercedes was parked near the curb. I still have a key that he gave me a long time ago, so I decided to surprise him, after all. I unlocked the door and slipped inside. But then, I heard laughter and voices that belonged to children. Stefan was sitting on the couch with my friend's portraitist and a small blonde girl. He was reading something to them in another language—I think it was English—and translated it into Polish. I had no idea he spoke in either of those languages. Besides Stefan's housekeeper, who was napping in the rocking chair, two more kids played with wooden toys on the divan. But what disgusts me the most is the way Stefan looked at that ugly portraitist.

When she called him Finn, I knew I'd been right from the very beginning. You see, Mutti, at the very beginning of our relationship, Stefan told me that he has an identical twin brother whose name is Finn. A couple of months ago, I noticed a change in Stefan's behavior. His eyes are warmer, and he courts me with a gentleness that contrasts with Stefan's harshness. I have been suspecting that Finn replaced Stefan. And I came to care for him the way I never did for Stefan, so I have been playing along with his scheme. My happiness is more important than the war. But Papa would never understand it, not like you. You are the only person I trust, Mutti.

I left without them noticing me. I must get rid of her. I haven't told Papa because I know how to fix this. Papa would kill him, and I can't imagine my life without him. Finn is mine; he just doesn't realize it yet.

But that's enough for now, as I have to continue packing for my trip. I want to hear from you, Mutti, so please write to me as soon you get this letter. Write to our address in Berlin.

I love you and miss you so much, my Mutti,
    Your Gerda

GERDA FOLDS the letter and kisses it. She wants so badly to hear from her mother.

One day Gerda found out her mother was aiding their Jewish neighbors, Ruth and Ira, by sheltering them in the basement. Without a second thought, she went straight to the Gestapo headquarters since her father was away. Her mother had broken the rules, and she needed to be guided back on the right track. The same day, the Gestapo showed up, and Gerda pointed out the Jewish people to them. She would never forget her mother's intense, cold stare. "That's not how I raised you, Gerda." Her voice was thick. Gerda's heart sank, and she wanted to stop the Gestapo men, but that would have been against the rules.

"Papa wants us to be faithful to the Führer, but you betrayed him," Gerda shot back. "I had no choice—it's for the good of all of us. Please forgive me, Mutti. I love you."

She stood there gazing at Gerda with her chin trembling and her lips pinched tight. She hadn't said anything else as they took her away. It pained Gerda so much to see her being taken away like that. It pained her to see this powerless disappointment in her mother's eyes.

Gerda didn't want to betray her mother because she truly loved her. But she knew she was genuinely doing the right thing.

Gerda thought her mother was unfair, but she had to finally realize that Gerda had saved her from sinking into a tunnel of crime. If her mother was hiding those two, she would be tempted to hide even more of those *sub-humans*, and then they would all be in trouble. Gerda had saved the reputation of the entire family. They should be grateful to her.

She stands up and walks to her father's study to find an empty envelope. She sees one on his desk, but there is a short telegram addressed to her father beneath it. She picks it up with caution, trying to chase away those black clouds that always come to her vision when she senses something terrible is going to happen. The telegram feels so heavy in her hands. She reads the central part of it aloud in a quiet but tense voice. "We are saddened to inform you of the passing of your wife, Anita Veicht, due to typhus complications on the twenty-eighth day of March 1944. Please accept our deepest condolences."

Gerda traces the words on the telegram with her fingers and sits for a long time, staring at them. Everything inside her is numb. She doesn't even try to stop those damn tears from forming; she just lets them come. The last time she cried was when she was a little girl, but she always had her mother for comfort, and now she is gone. She feels alone like never before. There was always a thought in the back of her mind that her mother would come back one day, but now everything has changed. She covers her face with her hands and sobs for a moment, which seems like an eternity.

She recalls many good moments spent with her Mutti. She had a perfect childhood thanks to her being always around.

When Gerda got older, though, she hated her mother for expecting her to be a good Samaritan.

When she was eight, a Polish couple with a daughter Gerda's age moved into their neighborhood. The girl's name was Hania. The family had been renting a basement apartment from Herr Bahn, the bakery owner. Gerda confessed to her mother that she felt bad for Hania, who wore simple clothes and had trouble connecting with other kids. Mutti suggested she tried to be friendly and talk to the girl.

Gerda set about doing something nice. With her mother's approval, she gifted Hania the red winter coat, the one from Aunt Martha. She didn't stop with that but always brought an extra snack to share. The girl seemed very grateful, and they became friends and hung out during school lunches and recesses.

Until one day, when Gerda came late to school to discover Hania had formed a friendship with another girl who had better grades than Gerda. It was hard to see Hania not paying attention to her anymore. She promised herself never to give her heart to strangers, as they were deceitful. She knew not to trust anyone anymore. Her mother's advice had been wrong.

On the other hand, her father was rarely home. Still, Gerda liked his views better, like the one about the German race's superiority. After all, she had learned the same things at school, and she had read and studied Adolf Hitler's *Mein Kampf*. That book had played an essential role in shaping her character and her ability to understand the world in the right way. She grew up to be a good German.

"You're not alone," Gerda whispers. "You still have Finn. You just have to get rid of that Polish whore."

18
Wanda

1 August 1944

A SMALL BOWL filled with blueberries sits on the kitchen counter. Mrs. Kowalska purchased it on the black market yesterday. Basia was so excited about helping make pierogi today. Maybe I should make them anyway? At least it will give me something to do, and they will fill Finn's stomach later.

Last night, Finn wasn't himself. When he held me in his arms while we were lying down in his bed, I couldn't help thinking that he held me as if it was our last time together. "Are you okay?" I asked.

He caressed my arm, his touch calm. "It's going to start tomorrow."

"What's going to start?" I asked, even though I knew very well what he was referring to.

"Witek calls it *powstanie*, uprising. It's going to be hell." He paused and stayed silent for a short moment. "Hitler won't leave until he burns down the entire city, and that works as well for Stalin. Only someone naïve would think otherwise."

"You think we are a bunch of fools for starting all of this?"

"No." He shook his head firmly. "I would do the same thing in your place. Five years of damn terror would have done it to me, too." His voice softened. "I'm just trying to be realistic, that's all."

"You're wrong. If the Soviets don't help us, other allies surely will." I couldn't see his face in the darkness surrounding us, but I sensed he disagreed with me.

"I already told Zuzanna to be up in the early morning to pack for herself and the children. I'm going to drive them into the country, where they can wait it out. I already spoke to my friend Ignacy, and he agreed to take care of them."

"What village?"

"Laski." He kissed the nape of my neck. I closed my eyes and took a deep breath, anticipating his next words.

"You should join them." The warmth of his breath lingered in my ear.

"I'm staying with you." I tried to sound calm. There was no way I was leaving.

"I can't stand the thought of losing you."

"My place is here. Don't fight me on this." I kissed his palms.

He sighed. "Then promise me you will be here tomorrow when I get back."

"I promise." I could promise him that one thing, but nothing else. I was determined to be a part of the uprising—some things were even more important than love—and even Finn couldn't stop me. But that conversation had to wait until the next day. He was exhausted, and I wanted him to have at least some sleep.

Now, I mix flour, salt, egg, and water until a smooth dough forms; then, I roll it out on the table. I have another hour before Finn stops by for lunch. I worry about how things went this morning. Was he able to drive Mrs. Kowalska and the children outside of Warsaw? If not, I'm sure I would have heard something by now.

The morning was so depressing. Mrs. Kowalska was up at five o'clock to pack. She kept saying that she was moving for the kids' sake; otherwise, she was ready to die where she belonged. Basia and Alek seemed to be excited about the prospect of a ride in Finn's car.

Tosia embraced me in a very long hug. "I will miss you," she said, tears flowing down her cheeks.

"I'll miss you too, sweetie. I'll see you soon." My heart felt like it was going to split in half. This girl tore at my heart, perhaps because she reminded me of myself—a lost soul.

I chase my memories away and using the mouth of a tin mug, I cut circles out of the dough. It's so familiar to feel the gnawing sadness that spreads through me. I keep telling myself that the children are safer over there. Who knows what will happen here?

I place a tablespoon of berries mixed with sugar on each round of dough, fold the dough over it, and pinch its edges to create a tight seal. After boiling the pierogi for about ten minutes, I place them on a dinner plate. I have another half an hour to spare before Finn is back.

"It stinks in here." I jump at the woman's harsh voice behind me. Gerda stands in the doorway with a pistol in her hand, a fake smile clinging to her crimson-red lips as she glares down at me.

"How did you get here?" This woman's presence intimidates me, but I confront her without blinking.

She utters a small, derisive laugh. "Stefan gave me a key. Anyway, I should ask you what you are doing here, fooling around with my fiancé?"

I'm too stunned to answer. I ache to tell her that her

murderous Stefan is, in fact, in jail and that Finn is only mine, but I know better. Her appearance intimidates me even more when she lowers her head and pinches together her eyebrows. She thinks I'm disgusting.

"I know what you have been doing, so I will get straight to the point, little whore."

"You have no right to call me that," I say, my stomach tightening.

"The Gestapo would do worse things to you. Is that what you want? Is that what you want for Finn?" Her eyes blaze with hate.

"I don't understand." My chest tightens.

"If you don't disappear within the next fifteen minutes, I will report Finn to the Gestapo for taking Stefan's place. In case you don't know, my father is a crucial figure in the Gestapo. He will believe every word I tell him, and that will be fatal for Finn. So, if you truly care for him, you must leave now and never come back." There is a dire warning in her tone.

I feel dizzy. How does she know about Finn? "What happens if I leave?" My voice sounds strangled, even to me.

"Then things will go as planned. I will keep the secret, and Stefan—I mean Finn—will leave with me for Berlin, where we will get married and live happily after." Her voice softens. "I love him more than anything, but if he can't be mine, he will die."

I don't doubt she intends to do just as she says. Finn told me how she denounced her mother. With a deep, shuddering breath, I gather my things. I have to leave before she summons Gestapo. I can't put Finn's life at risk. "I need to get a few of my belongings from upstairs," I say, hoping I can leave a hidden message for Finn.

"No need. You leave as you stand," she says, her voice firm.

"But first, you will write a note to *him*." She gesticulates with the gun to a pen and paper on the kitchen table, the same one I planned to use to write a letter to Mama and Kubuś.

19

Finn

I CAN'T WAIT ANY LONGER to see Wanda and assure her that Zuzanna and the children are safe. I'm so eager to leave my office and drive to her. I have to convince her not to participate in the upcoming uprising and instead let me take her to Laski. I can't bear to lose her. But she is a stubborn woman, and I'm afraid I won't be able to stop her. Worse, if I *do* stop her, she will never forgive me. I feel torn apart between the need to protect her and the need to understand her. The truth is I won't be able to stop her, just as she wouldn't be able to stop me, even though I love her more than anything. That realization tears at my heart.

The house smells good, with its fragrance of warmth and sweetness. But when I enter the family room, I stop dead in my tracks. Wanda isn't here.

My stomach churns. Gerda sits on the floral sofa, filing her nails. She looks up at me and puts on one of her wicked smiles.

"Hello, darling," she says, contempt in her voice. "Are you happy to see me?"

I'm so done playing games with her, but I have to be careful.

I'm sure Wanda is in hiding, maybe even listening to this conversation. She's fine, and I have to keep it that way. "Yes, of course. What a surprise." I walk toward her and peck her on the cheek.

"I knew you'd be happy," she says and pats her hand on the sofa. I take her hint and sit next to her.

"I came here because something urgent came up. Do you remember Fräulein Otenhoff's portraitist?"

My spine stiffens at her words. "Not really. Why?"

A flicker of irritation glints in her eyes. "Well, she visited my home this morning asking for Papa, but since he was at work, I assured her I would relay her message to him."

Her voice slices through my heart with the force of a knife. It takes all of my inner strength not to explode at her. "Why are you telling me this?"

Her face looks hard when her eyes rake mine. "Because she said that you are only pretending to be Stefan, and you are in truth his brother. Is that correct?"

I feel a sudden pain in my palms from my fingernails digging into the skin. "It's a lie," I say through clenched teeth.

"I didn't doubt it for a moment. So, I told the woman to get out and not to repeat such lies, or the Gestapo would take care of her." She gives a satisfied laugh. "She ran with her tail between her legs. I bet we won't see her anymore." She touches my cheek. "And don't worry darling, I won't repeat such atrocities to Papa, because I trust you. This woman was just jealous of our love. I noticed the way she looked at you in the Royal Bath Park when she was working on our portrait."

I have to play along with her scheme to keep Veicht out of this for as long as possible. "Thank you for trusting me, sweetie," I say, forcing a smile. This mission is compromised and has to be abandoned.

"I also came here with a message from Papa." Her face

wrinkles in contempt. "He wants me to move in with you here until I leave for Berlin. He says those Polish bandits will be starting trouble, and your villa is safer than ours. Is that fine with you, darling?"

I want to shout at her that no, that is not fine, but I smile with assurance instead. "Of course, darling. When are you planning to move in?"

"Tomorrow morning, as I need the rest of today to pack." Triumph gleams in her eyes. "Also, Papa thinks it's unsafe for me to travel alone to Berlin. He insists on you accompanying me."

Fury snaps through me. "He hasn't mentioned anything to me." What's going on here? Where's Wanda? Is she okay? There's no way she sold me away to Gerda. Someone else did. The first person coming to mind is Manfred. Maybe he's not so innocent after all.

"I asked him to let me tell you. But you don't seem happy at all," she says and places her hand on mine. "What's going on, darling?"

"Of course, I'm excited to accompany you. I've just had this terrible headache all day." This mission is over. I must find Wanda and escape.

20

Wanda

"I HAVE to go back there tonight," I tell Anna, who sits across from me at a small table at Café Anna, my painting of herbal roses directly in my view. I have a feeling Germans are aware of something significant happening today. Do they anticipate an uprising? How else to explain why the café, which is usually so crowded and full of life, is not busy today?

"You won't be able to do it tonight." She takes a drag from her cigarette, covers my hand with hers, and holds my eyes with hers. "Witek said the uprising is going to begin at five o'clock."

"I have to go. Gerda will make sure he reads the fake note she made me write." My mouth feels dry. I bite down on my bottom lip, unable to say the words that came into my mind. And when I do say them, my voice shakes. "He'll believe I don't love him."

She grabs my arm. "You need to calm down, Wanda. Finn isn't stupid. He knows Gerda, and he won't believe her. You need to have faith in him." She releases me and leans back in her chair. She takes another drag from her cigarette and exhales a cloud of smoke. A flicker of impatience mixed with compassion shines in her eyes.

I know she's right. I have to have faith in the man I love so much. So, why do I worry to such a degree? Because I don't trust Gerda, who is capable of the worst. Because I'm so afraid of losing him. Because I know that life isn't always as simple as black and white. I don't doubt Finn; I just doubt this unpredictable world; I doubt its cruel people. I can't control my worries.

"I'll try to get to him tonight," I say, a determination in my voice.

"It's too dangerous. It will all start within the next hour. It's going to be a nightmare, Wanda. Getting from here to Mokotów won't be possible, and I'm sure Finn wouldn't want you to risk your life in such a reckless way," she says with a sober expression. "Plus, who knows, Gerda may still be there. That deceiving bitch is on high alert today. She's making sure you're not coming back to him. Anyway, I wonder how she found out about Finn. He needs to get the hell out of there. According to the plan, he is to go into hiding once the uprising begins. His mission as Stefan is almost over."

"What should I do then?" I feel light-headed.

"Spend the night here, and tomorrow morning try to get through to Mokotów. I'm shutting down the café tonight for good and joining the uprising. But I'll go with you to Mokotów before that, just to make sure you're okay." She stubs out the cigarette in the ashtray. "What time does he usually leave for work in the morning?"

"Quarter to eight." I feel numb and heavy at the thought of not seeing Finn tonight, but I know Anna is right. I can't afford to be reckless anymore.

"We will be there at six." There's finality in her words.

"After I see Finn, I want to join you in the uprising. I have medical training so that I can be useful," I say. "We've been waiting for this for so long."

"I suspected that. I think you are doing the right thing." She looks around, and her gaze stops at the entrance, where a uniformed officer waves at her. He appears to be in his fifties. "I need your help entertaining that monster," she whispers, keeping her eyes on the stranger and smiling at him. "There are boys in the kitchen and backrooms getting ready for the uprising, and this man is very dangerous. He can bring an entire army of Gestapo down on us if he wants to."

I nod while feelings of dread overtake me. "What do you want me to do?"

"Try to draw his portrait, so he stays put and the boys can leave through the courtyard. Sometimes this man decides to take a peek into the kitchen, saying he's looking for me. Maybe he suspects something. He always comes alone and requests my company exclusively. He's an unsettling man."

She leaves me at the table and heads toward him. Once he is seated not far from me, Anna calls me over.

"Obersturmbannführer Veicht, this is my talented portraitist." She gestures toward me. "I have to warn you that she makes portraits only of the finest guests," she says. "So I'm leaving you in good hands."

His small, calculating eyes examine me. "Do I even qualify for such an honor?" Sarcasm folds his thin lips.

"I would never doubt that." Anna laughs. "Please excuse me for a brief moment. I must get ready for my performance."

After she leaves, he says with a trace of contentment, "Please, join me for a drink before we begin this boring assignment." He smirks, and I know this man is used to getting his own way.

Even though he acts friendly, I can't relax in his company, so I figure a drink might help me get through this ordeal.

He fills our glasses, but before lifting his, he says, "What would you like to drink to, Fräulein?"

I clear my throat, my insides shaking. "Of course for the success of the Third Reich," I say.

He takes my hand and kisses it, his eyes lifting to my lips. He looks pleased. Then he raises his glass and salutes to Hitler.

I copy him, suppressing my desire to spit in his face.

I begin to cough, and he smiles with pity. "I like smart women. Your German is impeccable." He takes a cigarette out and lights it. After exhaling clouds of smoke, he continues, "Just like your Aryan features."

"My grandmother was German," I lie, anxious for Anna to return so that I can start breathing again.

21

Finn

AFTER GERDA LEAVES, I race upstairs, hoping to find Wanda in hiding, but there's no sign of her. I don't doubt her innocence. There is no way that my sweet Wanda, who's so committed to the resistance that she let herself be tortured rather than giving up her contacts, would suddenly betray me. Gerda is lying. This evil woman orchestrated Wanda's disappearance from my life. I have to find her and make sure she's okay. I pray that Gerda didn't hurt her in any way. I decide to go to Anna, but first I walk around the house searching for a message that Wanda might have hidden for me.

After a brief search, I find a folded piece of paper on my bed tucked behind a pillow. My heart nervously jolts as I unfold it and recognize Wanda's handwriting: *I never loved you. This is wrong. I'm leaving you. Wanda*

Sweat beads suddenly on my forehead. I refuse to believe that the woman I love more than anything could be so deceptive. It must be one of Gerda's schemes. I have to find her, and I know the first place to check is Café Anna.

The moment I enter, I'm swallowed by cigarette smoke and

the sweet aroma from the kitchen that gives a gurgling to my stomach. As I walk toward the kitchen, I enjoy Mozart's *The Opera Don Giovanni,* so I pause to look at the pianist, but the moment I do, I freeze. Wanda and Veicht sit at the table across from me. He kisses her hand, and she smiles at him, and then they toast to the Third Reich. My heart sinks.

I instinctively walk backward so they don't see me and walk out of place. She not only sold me to Gerda but now also to Veicht. I must disappear.

Now everything makes sense. How else would Gerda have found out I replaced Stefan, if not from Wanda? Not from Manfred because if he were to betray me, he would go straight to Veicht's office. Wanda was too afraid to step into Szucha, so she went to Gerda instead and then found Veicht here.

She did it because of Stefan. She schemed to make me fall in love with her so that she could hurt me. When she saw what I felt for her, she betrayed me. And all of this to pay back for what Stefan did to her father.

I believed her when she said that I shouldn't apologize about Stefan's cruelty because we were two different people. She assured me that she didn't blame me for his actions. But all of this was just part of her game to kill me. I'm sure she expected Gerda to believe her and run to Veicht with the news, and when Gerda hadn't, she did it herself. She probably thinks I'm already dead by now. In truth, I wish I were.

I'm a man with a dead heart. Like an empty bottle thrown into the ocean, unable to be filled with love or trust. No, I'm more like a tree trunk—before, thriving with life; and now, missing its upper branches. I'm a wreck of a man determined never again to let anyone make me vulnerable.

22

Wanda

AT FIVE O'CLOCK in the evening, the streets are under artillery fire and bombardments. Unable to sleep at night, I listen with a soaring heart while staring into the darkness of Anna's flat. We have waited for this moment for so long. After five long years of terror, hope is seeded in our hearts again.

The next morning, despite the sleepless night, I feel refreshed from all the adrenalin. The plan is simple—meet with Finn to assure him of my feelings, warn him about Gerda's scheme, and then join the uprising. The rest is in God's hands.

On our way to Finn, we encounter running insurgents and couriers with white and red bands tied around their arms. Heavy gunfire never stops. People are building barricades out of anything. Some use wooden boards or house furniture. Others try to tear up cobblestones from the street using weird-looking iron tools.

We move forward, hovering near the buildings. The streets are covered with smoke from constant explosions. We finally manage to pass through the heat of the battles to Mokotów.

"Wait," Anna whispers and grabs my arm. "Let's wait here

and watch for a few minutes, just to make sure it's safe." We stand behind a wooden kiosk across from the villa.

Soon enough, a black Mercedes pulls in and parks next to the garden gate. A minute later, Gerda emerges from it. The gate swings wide open to reveal uniformed Finn. A rush of longing stirs through my body. But when Gerda runs toward Finn and throws her arms around his neck, my heart sinks. They kiss for a moment—a moment that seems to me like an eternity—while a couple of armed soldiers unload suitcases and trunks from the car. Gerda's luggage. She is moving in with Finn.

I feel Anna's hand on my back. "Don't take this the wrong way. Remember, he's on a mission, so he has to play along. He's just pretending to convince her not to give away his identity to the Gestapo."

Aware of streams of tears running down my cheeks, I don't look at her. "You are right. He's just saving the mission," I whisper, trying to convince myself. But there is a gnawing, empty pain spreading inside me. And then—just a numbness. "Let's leave," I say.

23

Wanda

25 September 1944

ANNA and I were separated right at the very beginning of the uprising. She was needed in the Old Town while I went to a hospital on Mokotowska Street where I worked as a nurse. Tata trained me in first aid over several summers before he retired, and it comes in handy now.

Like others, I believed that the uprising would last a couple of days. We waited for the Allies' help. But we were wrong. Now, after fifty-five days, we are nearing an utter defeat instead of liberation and political freedom.

While I'm on the go, I constantly feel Finn's presence. The thought of him gives me the necessary strength. I try to erase the memory of him kissing Gerda, as it slices through my heart. I repeat in my mind over and over that he was only fulfilling his mission, and he had to keep Gerda convinced. I don't doubt he figured out her scheme and didn't believe the fake note she forced me to write. He will find me once this awful war ends. We just have to survive.

There is never a dull moment in the overcrowded hospital. I tumble from one shift to another, feeling guilty whenever a commanding nurse forces me to take a rest. By now, the smells of lysine and rubbing alcohol are normal to me. Sometimes I wonder how it would be to live without them. But there are also things I never get used to, and one of them is the agonized moaning of the patients, heartbreaking sounds that go on through the days and nights.

We try to save as many as we can. Still, most of the time, they come to us in such poor conditions that the only thing we can do is hold their hands and help them through their painful transition to the next world.

"Wanda, Doctor Wrycki needs you in surgery," the red-haired nurse says as she rushes into the room. "He is about to do an operation on a boy we just admitted."

"Sure, but I'm not done here."

"Let me take over." She removes a bowl of broth from my hand.

"Thanks, Monika." I charge out of the room to find Doctor Wrycki.

The moment I see the gray circles under the doctor's bulging eyes, I realize how exhausted I am myself.

The bald doctor points to the patient on the operating table. "This boy was brought here unconscious with a very high fever from an infected wound. Probably a piece of a bullet is still inside it. Let's try to save him."

The moment I peer at the patient, my heart sinks. It's Jacek, the red-haired rickshaw boy. He looks very frail in the bright light that spills through the windows. "Will he survive?" I ask.

"I don't know. He is young, so hopefully he'll pull through," the doctor says in a weary voice.

I assist the doctor as he removes small pieces of bullet from Jacek's wound and stitches it up.

Over the next few days, his fever keeps spiking, and whenever he opens his eyes, he is unresponsive. A week later, however, when I stop by his bed I find him awake and aware. He stares at me with a trace of confusion, which soon changes to panic.

I touch his arm. "You are safe, Jacek. You are at the hospital."

"Miss Wanda?" he whispers. "Hospital? What happened?"

I touch his forehead. "Your fever is gone. You'll be fine." I smile at him. "There were leftover bullet fragments in your wound, and because of that, it got infected. Our doctor had to operate on you again. How are you feeling now?"

"I guess fine, just very thirsty," he says through parched lips.

I dash to the kitchen to fill a glass of water from the bucket and place it on a tray along with a bowl of *krupnik*, barley soup.

I nod with satisfaction when he drinks half the water. "Slow down. You don't want to go too fast and get sick again." I pick up the soup and spoon-feed him. "You're doing great, Jacek. Let's take a break now, and I'll come back later to feed you some more."

He shifts back into a lying position and sighs. "Thank you, Miss Wanda. I'm so lucky you are here."

I fix a blanket on him. "You are welcome. Get some more sleep now."

Just when I'm about to walk away, he grabs my arm. "I need to send a message to my family. They must be worrying about me." His pleading eyes tug at my heart.

"Of course. I will think of something, I promise—"

There is a sudden noise of running engines from outside. I clutch onto the iron frame of Jacek's bed.

A short moment later, a group of German soldiers charge in, machine guns in their hands. Soon they are followed by a heavy man in a gray uniform with the SS insignia. He paces around and says, "What a pigpen." Then he turns to his soldiers. "Shoot them all."

I freeze. I'm probably the only one who understands German, so there is no reaction from anyone else.

Just as the SS officer takes the first step toward the exit, Helmut, a wounded German soldier, says, "I'm a German officer, and I demand you rescind your command. Those people brought me back to health, and they don't deserve this."

The bulky officer turns back and gazes at the young German with a bandaged head. "Of course. I had no idea any of our people were here." He gives a half-smile. "Your wish will be granted, Officer."

I exhale with relief.

"But we do need everyone who can walk to gather in the courtyard, just for organizational purposes," he adds before walking away.

Helmut gets up and looks at me. "You will all be fine. I give you my word." He smiles at me. "Thank you for your care." He walks away.

The armed soldiers push confused people out of the room.

The wounded German saved us, but I still have a bad feeling about this. I grab Jacek's arm. "Come on, Jacek, you need to come with me."

He looks at me with his gaze wide. "I can't walk—I'm too weak."

"I will help you." The soldiers don't stop me from walking him out to the courtyard.

"What did that German soldier say?" Jacek asks.

"He saved our lives," I whisper, still feeling a surge of panic —what a dark, rainy day. I feel a hollowness in my chest. People stand with drooping shoulders and bent necks. Germans are so unpredictable that no one believes they will spare us. Everyone has heard about the massacres that happened in the Old Town after capitulation.

Then the waves of shootings, interspersed by short breaks, reverberate from the hospital as if soldiers are moving from room to room and mowing down everyone left behind. My heart bleeds. People cry and pray aloud.

I tighten my grip on Jacek, not knowing where to look or what to do. I feel guilty for not staying inside with the bedridden patients. I don't see Monika or Doctor Wrycki anywhere. Are they still in the hospital?

"It just can't be," Jacek whispers, and then he emits a strangled sob.

"We are next," someone in the crowd says.

Soldiers encircle us with machine guns, so no one tries to escape. That would be a death sentence.

I try to calm everyone. "Helmut, the German we cared for, asked them to spare us. I think this is why they told us to come here." After I say it, I feel my energy plummet. Who am I trying to convince? Myself or them?

It turns out I'm right. Soon the soldiers direct us toward the street and force us to merge with crowds of people leaving Warsaw. It's clear the uprising is over—and we have lost.

"Let me help you," Monika's voice comes from behind us. She takes Jacek's other arm.

"Thanks," I say, relieved to see her. "Have you seen Doctor Wrycki?"

She stops. There's a haunted look in her eyes that unsettles me. "He stayed with the others."

Her words tear through my broken soul. "Bastards," I whisper and wipe tears from my face.

I will never forget this rainy day. The city is absorbed in this sad silence that rips at my heart. My throat tightens as we leave behind the skeletons of buildings with empty windows and streets covered with cross-marked graves. The burned-down city has become a graveyard for so many. And then, there are the arrogant faces of the Germans who are supervising our departure.

We take advantage of the chaos and mix with the civilians on the way to the camp in Pruszków, where we spend the next couple of weeks, which is crucial for Jacek's recovery.

2 4

Wanda

Four weeks later, three kilometers from Tosaki

WE HAVE NO MORE strength to continue, so we stop in the birch forest near midnight. Jacek gathers some wood and starts a small fire. I pull a wool blanket around my shoulders, given to me by one of the villagers on the way here.

We have traveled on foot for almost two weeks now as we avoided the main roads and encounters with German soldiers. Now we are finally near our destination. The area is already free from German occupation, and I'm sure that the Soviets will not bother us.

I'm more concerned about my worsening health, as I've been feeling nauseous. I dread typhus or dysentery, but I put my worries aside and concentrate on getting to Tosaki, to my family.

I never feel alone. The thought of Finn is with me when I walk or eat or rest. I wonder if he is already in Berlin, as Gerda predicted. Most of all, I wonder if I did right by leaving without a word. At the time, I thought I had no choice and that I was protecting him, but now I'm not so sure. Why didn't I try to come back to him that night and explain what happened? Why didn't I at least sneak into the villa to leave a note? It's too late now, and it makes no sense to torture myself. When this awful war ends, he will find me.

This morning I woke up feeling sick to my stomach. I don't have the strength to even lift my head.

"Jacek, you must go for help. I'm very ill," I say.

He presses his hand to my forehead. "I can't leave you like this."

"We have no choice." I tell him where my family lives.

"Okay. Stay strong, Miss Wanda. I'll be back in no time." There is a note of assurance in his voice.

"It's only about three kilometers, but please, be careful," I say as he walks away. I feel exhausted, as if I have been lifting very heavy objects, so I fall back to sleep.

When I wake up, there is still no sign of Jacek, but I'm much better. I feel no more nausea, and I have most of my strength back. The wind has blown the blanket off me, so I wrap it around myself again until the warmth returns to my body. After eating some stale bread and drinking cold water, I decide to head toward the village. Maybe Jacek is in trouble. I wade through the tall grass of the birch forest and reach a dirt road. I'm not carrying much with me—just the wool blanket and some bread and water. Since the beginning of the uprising, I have worn the same clothes, and I can't remember when I last saw my face in a mirror. I've tried to wash in the rivers and lakes.

When I take another turn, I hear strange noises from the woods. I creep in that direction. A man in uniform leans above a woman, his pants down. The woman is sobbing and trying to get free of him. He mutters insults to her in Russian. Blood rushes to my brain. What to do? He is a big man, about six feet tall and with a solid build. I find a wooden stick, edge toward him, and press it to his back. He freezes but doesn't turn.

"Get to your knees and put your hands on the back of your head, or I will shoot you like a dog," I say in Russian.

"Bitch," he says but obeys.

I remove his pistol from the holster, place my finger on the trigger, and load the gun. "I will shoot your ass off if you make the slightest move." He reeks of vodka.

The girl lifts herself off the ground and adjusts her torn skirt. She is a pretty brunette. I'm surprised she doesn't run away that very moment.

I order him to undress. He curses at me several times but obeys before I let him ride away naked on his horse. Sadly, even that comical sight doesn't make me laugh.

"Are you okay?" I ask the girl, who seems frozen in place, watching me in awe. She is no more than fifteen or sixteen.

"Yes. Thank you." She pauses and looks at me with worry in her eyes. "Please don't tell anyone." Her face is red with shame.

"Of course, but you have nothing to be ashamed of. You are a victim of this brute."

"You are not from here," she says, appraising me. "You have no idea what has been happening." It's as if she is accusing me of something.

"No, but my family lives here."

She nods, tears coming down her cheeks. "I have been lucky so far, but today was a close call. This is all so unfair."

I move forward and embrace her. "I'm so sorry." A surge of anger tickles my throat. "What's your name?"

"Justyna."

"You are very brave, Justyna. I think you should avoid leaving home by yourself since it's so dangerous now."

"I have no choice. I live with my grandma only. Everyone else is dead," she says, her bottom lip trembling.

It turns out that she resides in one of the outbuildings that belong to my aunt. When we reach the dirt road, I spot a horse and wagon. To my astonishment, it's my aunt who is driving it; Jacek sits next to her. I'm so relieved to see them, to be able to hug my aunt. There have been moments in my life when I doubted I would see her again.

"I see you met our sweet Justyna," she says. "Let's take you girls home. It's been more and more dangerous lately for pretty girls like you to wander around on your own." She stares at Justyna, who blushes. "You won't believe me if I tell you we just saw a deviant on horseback, drunk and naked." She sighs. "This world is turning upside down."

I take a seat next to my aunt while Justyna and Jacek settle in the back of the wagon.

"Tell me, *Ciocia*, are you all okay?" I ask.

She snaps the reins, making the two horses move forward. "We are fine. Your mother and Kubuś are still living with us, but Mateusz left for Warsaw shortly after you did."

"He did?" I touch my throat. "Warsaw is burnt down. There is nothing to go back to."

She nods, her face covered with sadness. "He will be back soon; rest assured." Her voice is quiet. "He always loved it here, and he wants to move here."

Maybe my brother was in the crowds of people leaving Warsaw, just as I was. I let hope reassure me. He is alive; I feel it.

"How's Uncle Mirek?" I ask.

"Busy, as always. I don't know for how much longer, though. Our manor house is crowded with Soviet soldiers, and we heard rumors that they will be taking our lands away from us." She sighs. "We shall see."

"Oh, no." I feel weakness in my muscles. "How is that possible?"

"I don't know, honey, but they want to make everything public."

"You still live in the cottage, then?"

"Yes, for now. Your uncle and I are old, so we don't need much anyway. When Mateusz comes back, he will decide what to do." She speaks with assurance, so I leave it at that, but worries creep into my mind. Because of this awful war, nothing is ever going to be the same.

"At least you don't have to deal with Germans anymore," I say.

She gazes at me. "I don't know who is worse: Hitler or Stalin. I don't trust either of them, and you better be wary too. We are far from being a free country."

25
Wanda

"Doctor Kalowski, are you sure?" I ask the gray-haired doctor, who is busy packing his instruments into a black leather bag.

"Yes." His eyes evade me. He turns and walks away with slumped shoulders, but before opening the heavy oak door, he pauses and speaks with a pained expression on his deeply wrinkled face. "Were you forced?"

I'm not surprised by his question. "No. I love the man, and he loves me."

He sighs with noticeable relief. "Good. I had to ask. My hospital is flooded every day now with women who are victims of rape." He sighs again. "Take good care of yourself, young lady."

For the first time, I don't know how to feel. Sad? Happy? Both? I bury my face in a pillow. Someone knocks on the door, but I want to be left alone. The door swings wide open, and little Kubuś bounces his way onto my bed and lays his head on my chest. Maybe I don't want to be left alone, after all. Isn't it easier to go through things with loved ones? Time to stop running away; I'm not a lost teenager anymore.

"Kubuś, let Wanda rest." Mama's voice is soft.

"That's okay, Mama. Please, come in. I need to talk to you anyway." When I tell her about my pregnancy, she doesn't seem the least bit startled.

"I suspected when you kept having the morning sickness," she says, no sign of judgment in her eyes or voice.

"Kubuś," comes Jacek's voice from outside. Our little boy springs to his feet and is gone within seconds.

Mama is sitting on the side of my bed. "You've changed, Wanda. You have this peace in you now."

When I came home a couple of days ago, it was terrific to see Mama, but still, we hadn't talked about things. "Because I realize what matters in life." I smile at her before continuing. "And because of the special man who helped me find peace within myself. The father of my child." I tell Mama what has happened in my life since I saw her last. She listens with interest and sometimes a frown, but she doesn't interrupt me once. She has changed, too. The old Mama would have scolded me. I think losing Tata did it to her, and maybe caring for Kubuś.

"The way you talk about him..." Silence springs up between us, but it doesn't feel uncomfortable. "You love him." There is no accusation in her voice; it's just a statement.

I nod. "I dread not seeing him anymore."

"Things will work out, either way. They just have to. You will never be alone."

I move to a sitting position and put my head on Mama's lap. "I'm so sorry for the way I acted toward you."

"The best thing we all can do is to move forward. I understood you needed some time to let things settle. But I'm glad that you were able to move on and forgive me, forgive your father. We made some mistakes, but we always put you and your brother first."

My throat tightens. "I know, Mama."

"Your biological mother was a warm and friendly woman, and she loved you more than anything. It's not easy for me to say this, but it's the truth. There's not much I can tell you about her, but I do know where her parents live." She strokes my hair. "When times get more stable, I think you should visit them. I know now that we made a mistake by hiding it from you."

Talking to my mother is like applying a balm to my soul, something so lacking in our previous relationship. She makes me believe that things will eventually turn out just fine, that the baby is a gift to be cherished. I like that way of thinking. I'm tired of worrying about everything. It's time to move forward; after all, I'm lucky to be still alive.

Later, I write a short note to Finn. Even though I can't send it, just writing it makes me feel closer to him. It isn't my first note to him. I stack them under my mattress.

4 November 1944

Dear Finn,

I have something special to share with you—I just found out I'm expecting our baby. It seems so unreal that I keep pinching my ear. I have been feeling tired lately, and sometimes I get sick to my stomach, mostly in the mornings. That's all fine, though, because now I'm safe in Tosaki with my family. The Germans are gone.

My due date is in the middle of April, and I hope, with all of my heart, that by then, you will be with me. I can't wait until all of this ends and you are back. I believe you will find me, darling, will you not?

I have been having this strange feeling of your constant presence for so long now. It's as if you stay by me day and night, but still, I miss you so much.

I hope you often think of me, my love.

Your Wanda

26

Finn

June 1945, London, England

AFTER WANDA'S BETRAYAL, it was too dangerous to go on with the mission. Gerda and Veicht knew the truth. Gerda was young and naïve, and she believed I would go with her to Berlin, but she was also unpredictable.

That night I found Manfred, and we joined the uprising. I went back to the villa in the early morning, after making sure it wasn't under the Gestapo's surveillance. I grabbed a few essential things, and just as I was headed back out, Gerda's car appeared in the front of the garden gate, as if she were waiting for me. It was too late to back off, so I pasted a smile on my face, pretending to be thrilled to see her.

To my astonishment, she ran to me and kissed me on the mouth. When I saw her trunks being unloaded from the car, I knew she had found a way to deal with Veicht, so he had spared me. It made no sense, but at this point nothing could surprise me. The thought of how much she wanted me scared me to death. Maybe if Stefan had treated her with more compassion and spent less time in the brothels, she would have exposed me the moment she discovered my identity. For once, my brother's evil had served me well.

"What time you will be back, darling?" she asked.

"What time shall I return?" I folded my mouth into a charming smile.

She beamed. "As soon as you can."

After we said our goodbyes, I headed straight to the city center to Manfred and the rest of the insurrectionists.

Witek helped me transmit an encrypted message to London. I got a quick response to wait in the Kampinos on the fifth day of October.

We fought until capitulation on the third of October. About two hundred thousand inhabitants of Warsaw lost their lives— one of them was Witek.

Crowds of civilians abandoned the burning city and headed to the temporary camp in Pruszków, located along Warsaw's western edge. Hitler agreed to treat the uprising fighters according to the Geneva Convention, a peacetime agreement made in Switzerland in 1929. My blood still boils at the thought of how little trust one can have in the devil's word. What fate, in truth, awaited these brave and innocent people?

Manfred and I had to find a way to the assigned point in Kampinos. The fact that we had kept our uniforms in one of the safe houses in the city center and put them on right before the Nazis arrived allowed us to fulfill our plan. No one dared to question a captain, and I had no supervisor on my back.

While I watched the resistance fighters on their way out of Warsaw, I had an unceasing tightness in my chest. The war was almost over, but these people were traveling into the unknown. But then, they were the lucky ones, as there were way too many who had already paid the ultimate price.

An Armstrong Whitworth Whitley bomber picked us up

from Kampinos after a two-hour delay, but we arrived in London the next morning.

Now, eight months later, I'm still awaiting my trip back home. The British took full advantage of me, but now since Hitler is dead and the war is over, I'm flying to New York in three days. Manfred will go along thanks to the special visa I obtained for him, since he is still under eighteen and an orphan.

During our stay in England, thanks to our fluency in German, we were employed as *secret listeners*. We spent endless hours listening to the bugged conversations of German prisoners captured by the British. They lived in Trent Park, in homes-turned-prisons in north London. They drank wine and ate good food, and relaxed their vigilance. Glued to the bugging devices in the microphoned room, I grew bored listening to the bastards. I found out soon enough they had no idea we were spying on them, and thanks to that, we learned a lot of essential details that helped with the war effort.

I have to do one more thing before my departure. I have to see my brother. I need to look into his eyes once more to know if anything has changed in him. I need to know if he realizes the extent of his atrocities or if he is still proud of his actions. I will give him one more chance. I will make one more attempt to reach him.

I follow the guard into the maze of gates and cold hallways with cement walls, the heavy *click-click* of our footsteps echoing along the corridor floor. We pause in front of an iron door, and after the sound of a heavy set of jingling keys, the guard swings it open and takes his place to the side of the door. He refuses to leave.

My brother, dressed in prison clothes, sits at a small table fastened to the wall. He's reading something. He doesn't react when I walk in, as if he's used to visits from strangers. But I'm not a stranger, and I made sure he was informed of my visit ahead of time.

The metallic smell enters my nostrils. The walls are barren; the iron bed is neatly made; the small window is barred. The one word to describe this room would be *cold*.

I inch toward the table and take a seat across from him. He continues reading his book, not making a single gesture to acknowledge my presence.

"Hello. What are you reading?"

He snaps the book closed and tosses it to his bed. "What are you doing here?" he asks, his voice empty of emotion, just like this room. "I'm surprised you aren't living a life of luxury across the ocean." His face and his eyes are like iron. They reveal neither negative nor positive emotions, almost as if he has intentionally made himself unreadable to me.

My heart sinks; I have no more illusions. Just as he had done through our time growing up together, he rejects me now again by refusing to show any emotion. He's shielding himself with an iron mask.

"My life is no luxury. But I'm leaving tomorrow and just wanted to see how you're doing... and say goodbye." I know he has no idea I stepped into his place in Warsaw, so I hope that would make our conversation somewhat more manageable.

No reaction from him, just a disinterested look on his face. "Have you heard of this place called London Cage?" The way he asks his question gives away no sentiment. It's just a dull question, as if he doesn't care. Yet, I suspect he does care; that's why he wants to talk about it.

"I have." It's a facility where British agents interrogate the captured Nazis. It's unknown to public, but I learned about it because of my work for Intelligence.

"It's a beautiful place in Kensington Palace Garden," he says and utters a brief laugh. "Magnificent houses of torture."

"They took you there?" I don't feel pity for him because I know what he did on Szucha Avenue and in Warsaw's ghetto. What I learned about Stefan would instantly kill my mother, so I vowed to keep her in the dark and only tell her a little of the truth. "I don't see that torture has affected you in any way."

"They told me to abandon all hope. But they extracted nothing from me, nothing that would have affected the Führer and the Third Reich."

"The Führer is dead. The Third Reich is dead." There is a finality in my words, but it makes no difference in Stefan's blank facial expression. He has assumed his mask well enough to isolate himself, to not let me in. But since he mentioned Hitler, I have a hint of what could be going on inside him. He is still the same Stefan.

I swallow hard. "It seems as if it doesn't make any difference to your beliefs. You are still taking that evil path." After a few moments of silence, something snaps in me. "Goddammit, Stefan. Talk to me."

"Time is up," the guard's voice rings out.

Stefan stretches his arms and yawns. "He's right. It's dinnertime, and I wouldn't miss it for the world. The best thing about this boring dungeon is that they give you decent food. Not bland at all." He stands up and reaches for something from beneath his mattress. "Here, I wrote you a letter. It will answer all your questions. I'm not as good a talker as you are, but I'm a better writer. Open it when you get home and read it in peace. Make sure to read it carefully, every word. Because every single word I wrote is how I feel. It's the ultimate truth I believe in."

I make intense eye contact with him, but there is still nothing. Maybe this letter, indeed, will shed more light on my brother's emotional state. I take it from his hand and slip toward the door, resisting the strong desire to hug my brother, despite his choice to cut me off. Despite everything.

"Tell Mutter that I'm homesick," he says.

* * *

I can't bring myself to open Stefan's letter. I'm so afraid of the ultimate truth about my brother, and I have a feeling this letter explains it all. As Stefan said, it contains the final answers I need to move on with my life.

I'm still hurting after Wanda's betrayal. The woman to whom I gave my heart, with whom I was vulnerable. I spent many nights awake thinking of her, analyzing her every gesture, remembering her every word. Looking for a clue that should have made me aware of her treacherous intentions. I found nothing. Maybe she was as good as Stefan when it came to hiding under a mask of detachment, and in Wanda's case, a master of pretense. That's all it was with her: acting. I'm still mourning her betrayal, getting ready for the next step: anger.

I open Stefan's letter in the middle of the night. There are only five words written in large lettering: *Be ready to die soon.*

No remorse or empathy, just those words of hatred toward me. My heart bleeds, but my mind sobers for good when it comes to my brother. And when it comes to Wanda.

27

Wanda

21 September 1945

Warsaw, Poland

WE FIND our house in Żoliborz untouched, although most of Warsaw is in ruins. When we come back from Tosaki, my daughter Kalina has just turned four months. My heart leaps with joy every time I look at her. She has Finn's eyes.

The house needs a lot of cleaning, and at first, there is no electricity. However, Mama has been bursting with energy, so in no time, we sort things out. I love seeing her so happy, and it crosses my mind so many times that Tata must be proud of her. Kubuś is the one who brings a smile to her face every day. He gleams like sunshine in our lives.

A week after we arrive back, I go to visit Mrs. Kowalska in Mokotów. I find her in the backyard washing children's clothes while all three of them play outside. They run toward me and hug me for a long time before returning to their play. Tosia shows me the new book she has been reading, *Emily of the New Moon* by Lucy Maud Montgomery. She stays with us for a while, chatting about her dreams to become a writer one day. I enjoy listening to her happy chatter. Whatever the older lady has been doing is working.

I help Mrs. Kowalska with the laundry, both of us on our knees rubbing clothes in the basin filled with water and soap. She hasn't changed a bit since I saw her last time—still the same cheerful and warm lady with gray hair and wrinkles on her wise face.

We remain in silence for a while, and the sound of rubbing fabric competes with birds' singing and children's excited voices from the adjoining garden.

The lazy sunshine caresses my skin and hair—it's the kind of day that can lift moods. "What are your plans?" I ask.

"My daughter wants us to move to Canada, and she is already working on it. If we get visas, it will be a chance for a better life for the children."

I can't argue with her. Life in communist Poland isn't easy, especially for people who fought in the resistance. People accused of espionage disappear daily, being tortured or killed. Mrs. Kowalska is making the right decision to try to emigrate.

"I hope everything works out," I tell her.

"I hope so, as I'm not getting any younger, and those rascals need a lot of care. My daughter is planning to adopt them." There is a somber expression on her face. I wonder if she is thinking about her deceased son right now, but she surprises me by changing the subject.

"Are you in touch with Finn?" she asks.

I clear my throat. "No, he never contacted me." It's hard to admit it, as if saying it confirms that Finn moved on in his life without me.

A frown clouds her face. "Well, I hope he survived, and I'm

sure he will get in touch with you when he can. After all, his mission was very dangerous."

I don't want to tell her that I have already lost hope, so I lift a white t-shirt and busy myself examining it for hidden stains.

She doesn't relent. "You should try to find him. Who knows what scheme that charlatan of a woman pulled upon him?" She rinses the last shirt in clean water and wrings it. "That boy would give his life for you."

After we finish the laundry, we hang it on the lines stretched between trees and go inside to have lunch. I enjoy delicious *naleśniki z serem*, crepes with curd, while the house brings memories of time spent with Finn.

My heart fills with emotion. I should inform him about our daughter. What will I say to him, though? *I know you don't want me anymore, and to be honest, at this point, I'm not sure if you ever wanted me. Maybe for you, it was just a wartime affair, and you don't even remember it. But things are a little more complicated than you expected them to be.* No, I wouldn't say that to him. It would sound as if I were trying to awaken a feeling of pity in him.

Before I leave, I promise Mrs. Kowalska to come back next time with Kalina and Kubuś.

* * *

I take a trolley to the Royal Bath Park in the city center. In her black jumpsuit, Anna is waiting for me in an open-air amphitheater on the east bank of the south pond of the park. She's sitting on a bench facing a narrow strip of the pond with the scene guarded by a stone monument of a lion.

The sun gleams on the water, increasing the familiar smell of earth and decaying algae.

"Here you are." I take a seat next to her. "Sorry I'm late." She has a stern look on her face. "You seem angry."

She sighs. "No, I'm just tired."

"You need to do something about your lack of sleep," I say.

A thin smile edges her lips. "Not that kind of tired. I'm just tired of the world we live in," she says, folding her arms, her gaze focused on the scene before us. "I was thrilled after the war to go back to acting, but it's been worse than I anticipated. They keep forcing me to perform in those awful political plays. If I refuse them any longer, I will end up in the *UB*, Department of Security, jail."

"That's not good. If they find out that you were in *Armia Krajowa*, they will surely go after you."

"I know, but I can't do what they want me to, so I'm leaving before it's too late."

My breath catches. "Where are you going?"

She rests her hand on my arm. "I'll be fine. I have it all planned out." For a moment, we listen to deep, trumpeting sounds from the swans in the pond, as if they just approved Anna's decision.

"When?"

"Tonight." She scans the surroundings and says in a voice so low that I hardly make out her words, "I'm going to Tosaki."

I feel a knot forming in my stomach. "Why Tosaki?" I whisper, unable to control my inner panic.

She lifts her hand off my arm and tugs a strand of her blond hair behind her ear. "I want to convince Mateusz to leave with me for England. He can't live like this. They will eventually capture and kill him."

She is right. After the war, my brother, like many other resistance fighters, refused to submit to the Soviet-driven government and remains in the woods fighting them. We keep trying to convince him to resume a normal life and open his doctor's practice again, but he argues that the *UB* would arrest or kill him like many others if he didn't remain in hiding. I can't argue with him because, deep inside, I know he is right.

"I agree, but my brother is so stubborn. And I can't say he is wrong in what he is doing, but it's so obvious he has no chance."

"Exactly. I want him to stay alive."

"If there is anyone who can convince him, it's you. I've noticed the way he looks at you." I sigh. "If only he weren't so damn headstrong."

Anna and Mateusz met again during the uprising as they were both assigned to fight in the Old Town. Right before capitulation, thinking they were all going to die, he confessed his true feelings to her and that he had been in love with her for so long. In the end, they were able to escape through the underground sewer and survive.

"I guess we're a good match then." Anna laughs with delight.

I smile at her. "I will write a letter to my aunt so that you can stay at their house. I know Mateusz often visits them."

She sags against me. "This is why I love you so much, my friend."

"I will miss both of you, but I know it's all for the best, and I pray this will work out." My eyes fill with tears. "My brother is lucky to have you. You are his only hope."

She sighs. "I wish he thought the same way you do." She draws her eyebrows together. "You should come with us too. I have connections, so there will be no problem obtaining visas." She searches my face. "I'm serious, Wanda. What if one day they find out about your past in the resistance and decide to harass you?"

"I have been keeping a low profile, so I'm not really a target for them." I take her hands in mine. "But I do appreciate you thinking of me."

"Then at least try to find Finn and inform him about Kalina. He is not going to reject his daughter, and any help is good."

A lump comes to my throat. "I don't need his help, but yes, I should inform him that he has a daughter. I don't want to make my father's mistake." Every person I meet with today tells me to find and contact Finn. Don't they see that he chose for our paths not to cross again? *You must think of Kalina,* a voice inside me says.

That night I can't stop thinking of what Anna said about Finn. She is certain he would accept his daughter, but would he believe Kalina is, in truth, his? How would he react to that news? Would he try to take her away from me or apologize for not returning to me? After all, I don't need to worry about it because there is no sign of Finn, and I don't even know how to find him.

I have more pressing concerns to address, like the one about our finances. We have been receiving tremendous help from Aunt Krysia and Uncle Mirek. Still, it's time I found a job and became independent.

Over the next couple of weeks, I look at job announcements. Going on interviews turns out to be even more discouraging. The money offered is so little that it wouldn't be enough to feed and pay bills for four people.

One day, my hopes soar. The job advertisement I find in the newspaper is for a translator's position at the American Consulate. I didn't finish my studies at the University of Warsaw, but I plan to do that soon. I need to show them that I'm fluent in English.

When I arrive at the consulate, a goateed young man greets me. He is initially very reserved, but he relaxes when I mention that I'm an artist. We talk about that for the rest of the interview, as he too loves to paint.

It takes almost a month before receiving a phone call with a job offer for a translator position. I can't stop smiling. Finally, faith rewards me for my endurance and perseverance.

I enjoy my job, and the pay is decent. I meet many interesting people, most of them from abroad.

The wound left by Finn is slowly healing. I have to come to terms with his rejection, with the fact he chose someone else over me. I hope it isn't Gerda; just the thought of her gives me goose bumps. My heart tells me it isn't the case, though. Finn was disgusted with her behavior. What happened during the war was just to ensure the success of his mission.

And then, there is this worry that maybe, after all, the mission was not a success, and he is gone. I swallow hard. No, it has to be something Gerda did that made him not contact me again. I refuse to believe he would have decided based on that silly letter Gerda forced me to write. Not Finn. He is too wise to succumb to her manipulations. So what was it that took him away from me?

I have to stop dwelling on this and accept it. Yet, there is still the gnawing question of his knowledge of Kalina. Will my daughter ever forgive me if I don't at least try to find him, so she knows her father? I would give so much to have Tata back, to meet my biological mother and get to know her. Kalina still has a chance for a relationship with her father.

28

Wanda

8 May 1946

Warsaw, Poland

Dear Finn,

First, I would like to express how happy I am to learn you are safe
with your family in New York. That mission of yours was a
dangerous one.

I'm writing to inform you that our daughter Kalina was born on
April 21st, 1945.

I'm not doing this to force you to acknowledge her, but I believe
it's right that you know of her existence. I will respect your decision
as to whether you want to be a part of her life.

Please contact me to let me know.

Sincerely,

Wanda Odwaga

I'M ENJOYING the intense aroma of coffee I just poured into a mug. It's challenging to write such a brief, neutral letter to Finn, but I believe it's the right thing. I don't know his motivation, why he chose to ignore me after the war. He doesn't need to know that I'm still not over him, that the wound is still fresh. I don't need his pity. If he decides to be present in Kalina's life, then perhaps we could resolve things between us and find peace for the sake of our daughter.

"Who are you writing to?" Mama's voice snaps me from my thoughts. She lumbers toward me and takes a seat at the kitchen table across from me.

I fold the letter and place it in an envelope. "Paul, the vice-consul, promised to help me send a letter to Finn. I want him to know about Kalina."

She puts her coffee down. "Are you sure about that?"

I frown, then shrug my shoulders. "Of course I'm not, though I believe it's the right thing to do."

"What if he decides to take her away from you?" she asks, a look of concern flashing over her face. For the moment, she sounds so negative, like my old Mama again. "I'm sure he has money and connections while we struggle every day to pay the bills. I think you should reconsider it."

I trace the edge of the coffee cup in front of me. "It did cross my mind many times, Mama, but the Finn I know would not do that. He is such a genuine and compassionate man." I study the red gingham tablecloth patterns as if trying not to pay much attention to Mama's worries.

"You don't know him, sweetheart. The fact he hasn't contacted you since the end of the war tells me everything about him." She reaches out and takes my hand. "I'm just worried, that's all. You will do what you think is right. I just don't want you to make the biggest mistake of your life. That little girl means everything to you, and to us."

I can't argue with her. She has a good point about my not knowing Finn that well. After all, our time together was brief, and war makes people behave differently. We were under constant fear of exposure at any time. Maybe that's why he reached out to me. Too bad my heart still leaps at the mere thought of him. I truly fell for this extraordinary man, and it pains me that he never found me again.

"My heart tells me to contact him. Besides, I don't want to make Tata's mistake. I want Kalina to know her father, even if I will never be with him." I gaze into her eyes. "You should understand that more than anyone else, Mama. Didn't you disagree with Tata about keeping me in the dark about my biological mother and grandparents?"

Her face wears a somber expression now. "Like I said, in the end, it's your decision and risk." She moves her hand from mine. "I meant to ask you about your grandparents. Did you go to the address I gave you?"

"I did, but it doesn't exist anymore." I take the last gulp of my coffee.

She creases her forehead. "What do you mean?"

"The building was bombed and knocked down during the uprising. According to the Red Cross, none of the tenants survived." I wipe away my tears. "They died hiding in the basement."

She surges from her seat and envelops me in a long hug. "I'm so sorry, darling."

My biological mother was their only child, so there is no more immediate family to look for. I have been searching for any extended relatives, but I have had no luck so far. I'm determined not to give up because I hope to learn at least a little about my birth mother.

Mama doesn't know much, and that is understandable. "That's okay, Mama."

She pats my back, picks up my empty coffee mug, and moves toward the kitchen stove. "Are you hungry?" she asks.

"I'm fine. I have to get going. I hate being late for work." I climb off my seat and move toward the door.

She holds my arm. "There is one more thing I need to talk to you about," she says.

I glance at my watch. "Can it wait until later? I really have to go."

"Yes, but it's about Kubuś," she whispers, even though both children are still asleep. "You should consider adopting him."

The Red Cross was not able to locate any of Kubuś's relatives. "I'll look into it. He has to stay with us." I smile at her. "I will make sure he does, Mama."

Part III

"The true love is when you get to know the other person so well that you can read his mind; when you support each other in your struggles; when you gain strength from being together in the most challenging moments, or even in ordinary situations." ~Wanda Odwaga

29

Finn

Three years later

Manhattan, New York

"HERE IS YOUR MAIL, FINN," says Nancy, my gray-haired secretary. She's like an aunt to me.

I smile. "Thank you, Nancy." After my Grandpa retired, I was pleased to see that Nancy was not eager to leave. She claims that working keeps her feeling younger.

"Happy birthday, my boy. I remember when you first came to this country. I believe you were only fourteen or fifteen." She cocks her head to the side as if she is trying to remember my exact age. "Both of your grandparents were so happy." She sighs. "Time flies."

"It does fly, but you still look fabulous." I stand up and walk around my desk to hug her.

"You get your charm after your Grandpa." A smile flickers on her lips. "Call me if you need anything."

After Nancy leaves, I sort through my mail, and there it is—the same letter from Germany I have been receiving on my birthday every year since the end of the war. No sender's name or address on the envelope. I don't need one. Even though the letter is anonymous and the handwriting is unfamiliar, I know it was sent by my brother.

I don't even need to open it to know the exact words. The four short sentences I could repeat in my sleep: *The day of sweet revenge is coming. You will beg for my forgiveness, but there will be none. You deserve none. Consider yourself dead.*

Nothing else. No name, no greeting, no date. Just those hurtful words to wish me a *happy birthday*. To remind me that my brother never regretted his atrocities. To remind me that the prison has made him even more evil. The truth is, I feel no connection to him. And no, I don't fear him; he disgusts me. The sorrow I felt for him for so long disappears when I read his letters. I have stopped mourning him. I accept there is no good-natured side to Stefan. Mother and I tried for a long time to awaken something good in him, but we failed.

30

Finn

July 9, 1949

Montauk, New York

I HAVE SPENT five years hating and loving a woman on the other side of the Atlantic. The woman who made me vulnerable, the woman who betrayed me.

After the war, I never bothered to check if she'd survived; somehow, I knew she must have. Instead, I spent every single day battling her, eager to purge her from my memories. I refused to dream about her, and I dated women who looked nothing like her. But I failed, and I knew it every morning when I awakened from my dreams—at first soothed by memories of her sweetness and then shaken by her betrayal. It didn't matter whom I woke up next to; she was always there, thriving in me. Surrounded by crowds of people, I was alone in my hate and love, alone in my pity. I was sure of one thing, though—our paths would never cross again.

But only until now.

I lift my head to look for a waiter with a tray of champagne, but instead, I see a breathtaking blonde in a sapphire dress, her eyes the color of a stormy-blue ocean. Wanda.

My first instinct is to refuse to believe the truth of what my eyes see—it can't be her. Time seems to slow down, and everyone else disappears—she is the only one in my view. She isn't as gaunt as I remember her; now, her body has delicate, feminine curves. Part of me yearns for her while the other remembers only her betrayal. I focus on her face to trace the signs of treachery, but find none, and that tears at my heart, bringing back the memory of seeing her for the first time.

I want to run to her and shake her with all my might. I want to cry out the one question that has been gnawing at my heart since the day she betrayed me: *Why?*

But I remain frozen in place while she laughs at something a lanky, black-haired man with a goatee whispers in her ear. The instant jealousy poisons my heart.

31

Wanda

THE SCENTS of seafood and cigarette smoke fill the air of the
Island Club on Lake Montauk. People's voices and laughter
mingle with the *clinking* of glasses. Gentle music circulates to a
singer's sensual voice. He sings about love, strangers, and
enchanted evenings. It's all so very foreign to me, but I still
enjoy the evening, taking it all in.

Once the party is in full swing, my fiancé Paul and his
friend Tony head to the gambling tables, leaving me with
Tony's wife, Louise. She turns out to be cheerful company. The
couple lives in New York City, so the woman knows well
tonight's circle of wealthy people. She introduces me to many
of her acquaintances, with whom we make small talk. I feel like
a little duckling in a circle of glorious swans, but I paste a smile
on my lips and take Louise's lead.

The lost hope of spending the night dancing away with my
fiancé leaves a sour taste in my mouth and melancholy in my
heart. I met Paul three years ago at the American Consulate,
where I provide translation services. It wasn't love at first sight,
but he was respectful, caring, and constant in showing me

affection. We shared a passion for painting, and that helped us to bond when we first met. I so admired his talent. After a year of dating, I agreed to marry him, even though we are more friends than lovers.

Mama keeps telling me that the meaning of true love is more complex than first enchantments. That true love is when you get to know the other person so well that you can read his mind, when you support each other in your struggles, when you gain strength from being together, either in the most challenging moments or in ordinary situations.

I hope to have that kind of relationship with Paul one day and experience the true meaning of love, although my heart has never healed after Finn. Deep inside me, my sacred feelings for Finn still flicker, despite his rejection.

When Paul informed me that he planned to go back to his home in New York for a couple of weeks, I was happy for him. It's a hard thing to be separated from your closest family. He asked me to go with him, and I agreed, even though he was clear that my four-year-old daughter would not go with us. He thought it best that she stayed safely at home with Mama. Later, I found myself regretting this decision because I felt miserable after only a few days of separation. I have one more week before I can be on that plane, on the way back to my daughter.

After spending almost a week with his family, Paul has booked a five-day stay in Montauk, far east of New York City, at the very tip of Long Island. We are staying in Montauk Manor, a charming hotel that looks like a castle on a hill.

"I know the men are playing golf tomorrow, so if you are free, come join the other ladies and me at the Cabana Club," Louise says and takes a sip of champagne. She is in her forties, but the age difference between us is hardly noticeable. Her tanned skin is complemented by her emerald cocktail dress, making her look youthful and fresh. She moves with grace and lightness, and she has the bright spirit of a firefly.

"Sounds good to me."

She nods with approval. "Do you mind if I ask how you met Paul?"

"We both work in the consulate in Poland," I say.

"That's interesting. How long have you been dating?"

"For almost a year, but we've known each other for over three years."

She nods. "That's not long." She gives me a meaningful look. "Don't rush to get married. It's good to know the other person for a long time before saying your vows."

The fact that she doesn't praise Paul surprises me. "Do you speak from your own experience?" She reminds me of my dear friend Anna, who is now married to my brother, Mateusz.

A brief laugh erupts from her. "Of course not," she says, opening her eyes wide like some excellent idea just struck her. "I just realized there is someone else here who speaks Polish." Without waiting for my response, she takes my hand and leads me through the crowded room, at some point whispering in my ear, "I've noticed him glancing many times in our direction tonight."

We approach a circle of two couples, who seem to be engrossed in their conversation. Louise touches the arm of an average-height but nicely built man in a tuxedo, who immediately turns our way. "Finn, I would like to introduce you to someone special," she says.

My heart stops for a split second, and then every fiber of my body is taut with astonishment. Finn. The man who chose not to return to me. The man who rejected his own daughter.

"Hello, Finn." I smile faintly.

He remains silent while his intense stare holds me captive. It suddenly feels as if there is no one else in the room. Yet, his eyes also reflect anger and conflict, as though he is fighting something powerful within himself.

I don't know how long we remain in that frozen moment, but a tall brunette puts her hand on Finn's arm and says, with a possessive look on her face, "Finn, you promised me this dance."

He nods, stone-faced, and they walk away. Just like that.

My cheeks burn. He said not a single word to me. His callous attitude makes my insides hurt, and I burn with embarrassment that transforms into fury. I so hate him.

Louise gives me a perplexed look but gently squeezes my hand. "You okay, honey? I had no idea you two knew each other."

I fight back hot tears and try to give her a reassuring smile. "Yes, we met a long time ago. He wasn't such a jerk back then, though." I roll my eyes. "Now, if you'll excuse me, I'm going to head into the powder room before Paul returns." I wink at her.

"Of course."

* * *

I pass by the powder room and slip outside. The waves of fresh, salty air fill my nostrils and ease my anxiety. I settle near the railing on the deserted veranda, watching the lake's rocky shoreline. Louise told me this is a saltwater lake connected with the ocean. The sound of music from inside and the sound of water striking the shoreline give me an impression of being trapped between two worlds.

At a far distance, a faint light rotates on a high point of land. It must be a lighthouse leading sailors safely to their destinations. I so need that guiding light in my life, especially now, when meeting Finn had crushed the inner world that I've built so carefully for so many years. I so despise that man, who just managed to discard me in front of other people as if I'm the one who wronged him. I would be surprised if Louise hasn't already spoken to Paul about it. I dread coming back inside, but I don't want to appear rude by leaving without saying goodbye. I sigh and gaze at a dark sky lighted with stars.

"Wanda." He says my name in a deep, husky voice that seems to vibrate along my nerves. He is so close. I feel his warm breath on the back of my neck.

I don't turn to him, afraid I might lose control and punch him. "Go away, Finn." My voice is harsh, exactly how I want it to be.

He grabs my arm, maneuvering me into his embrace.

Fury snaps through me, but his grip is so firm, I can't budge. "Let go of me, you bastard."

He half-smiles, his eyes fixed on my mouth.

I jerk my head back. "I will—"

"Why do the most beautiful women tend to be so deceitful?" His voice switches into a rough whisper.

"How dare you."

He lets out a small mocking laugh. "The truth always hurts."

"Damn you, let go of me. You aren't worth my time." I put a note of finality in my voice.

He keeps his grip strong; his stare fixed on me. "Oh, that's right. I'm boring because you can't dupe me this time." He smiles down at me with a hint of suspicion in his pale gray eyes and releases me. "Who's that goatee guy you came with?"

His choice of words angers me. Deceitful? Duped? It's time to end this conversation and make sure not to see him again. "The handsome man I'm deeply in love with is my fiancé. But it's not any of your business."

He glances at my small gold ring with a yellow sapphire, a mocking look on his face. "I guess you aren't worth diamonds."

I force myself to laugh and look him straight in the eye. "I care less for diamonds because what I have with Paul is beyond physical value." I don't care that I'm lying to him. I'm determined to hurt him the same way he hurt me. "Something you were never able to give me."

The moment I say it, something inside me snaps, and I feel drained. I don't want to fight anymore, even if he keeps insulting me. I also don't want to go back inside. I'm tired of pretending. Pretending to Paul, Louise, and all the people in there who don't give a hoot about me. I ache for home, for the difficult life I have over there, because it's mine, and I don't have to pretend. At that very moment, I decide to break up with Paul, whom I don't really love, and never again see or think about Finn.

I march toward the bridge. I know the way to the hotel, and it will probably take me no longer than an hour to walk there. So I do it—I leave Finn without saying a damn word.

"What do you think you're doing?" I'm surprised by his panting voice behind me. I've been walking for a few minutes toward the bridge, so he must have been running after me.

"It's not any of your business. Go away," I say without slowing down. I'm thankful it's still early and not so dark out.

"You can't just walk alone like that. It's too dangerous." His voice is shaking with anger.

"Stop snapping at me. The only dangerous thing here is your company." I give him a disgusted look. "It's an insult to me."

His hands clench into fists. "What a spoiled bitch you are."

I swallow hard. This one word slices through my heart with the force of a sharp knife. Somehow it hurts to hear it from him. Tears sting my eyes, but I turn and walk away, and he doesn't follow.

It takes more time than I had anticipated crossing the

bridge, but I'm hoping to have no more than forty minutes of walking ahead once I'm on the dirt road.

There is no sign of Finn. I feel an unexpected release of tension. It's becoming darker with every minute, so I increase my pace. My slippers hurt my feet, so I take them off, but the road is so rocky that I put them back on.

I dream of being in my bed, lost in soft covers. A good sleep always makes things easier for me and helps me refocus, and that's what I need.

"Look who we have here." A rough male voice comes from the woods on my right. A tall, young man jumps in front of me, a pocket knife in his hand. His hair is disheveled and his face is soiled with dirt, but his red eyes scare me the most.

He smirks at me, exposing his rotten front teeth. "Never expected to meet such a beautiful woman alone in these woods." His breath reeks of spirits. "Perhaps you have some cash that you would like to share with me?"

My throat tightens. "I don't have any." I wish I did have money, though, so he would take it and leave.

His face darkens as he moves even closer to me. "Open your purse," he says, gesturing with his knife.

My stomach muscles harden at his glare. I open my purse with shaking hands. He searches through it, tossing my lipstick and other accessories to the ground. It was a good decision not to bring any personal documents with me.

"Take off that necklace and ring," he finally says in a threatening voice.

"Fine, take them. I don't care about them, anyway." I gasp when I realize I've just shouted at him.

At that exact moment, Finn's calm voice comes from behind me. "Leave this lady alone." He followed me, after all. I sigh with relief.

"Mind your own business, man," the drunkard says and moves his knife in Finn's direction.

"Just take the damn jewelry and leave us alone," I tell him.

"He isn't going to take anything. He's going to apologize for his behavior," Finn says with a stern expression on his face.

The man gives a short but nervous laugh. "Get lost."

"Right, get lost." I glare at Finn and then turn to the other man. "And you take the damn jewelry and end this circus." I throw it at him.

In the same moment, Finn lunges at him, and everything happens so fast that the next thing I see is Finn's hand around the man's neck while his other hand grips the knife.

"What are you going to say now?" Finn's deep voice vibrates along my nerves. "Apologize to the lady, or I will cut your tongue out."

I swallow hard, believing him.

"I'm... I'm s-sorry," the man stutters.

"Now, you are going to walk into these woods and never again assault any passersby. Understood?"

By the time the man recedes into the woods, I have managed to gather my composure. "I didn't need your help. I was okay handling this myself." I glare at him. "What are you doing here anyway?"

"You're welcome," Finn says with heavy sarcasm.

"Fine, thank you, but now you can go back."

"No way. I'm walking you to the hotel." His arms crossed.

"Suit yourself." I pick up the items from the ground and replace them in my purse. I'm exhausted, but I keep up a steady pace, hoping to get to the hotel soon.

We walk the entire time without a word, and when we near the hotel entrance, I wipe the sweat off my forehead and place my still trembling hand on the doorknob. I don't want to say anything further to Finn.

"Typical," he says, with a note of insult in his voice.

I turn back to him. "Don't you dare try to insult me again," I say through a scowl. "Just do me a favor and stay out of my way."

He crosses his arms. "Not until you pay for your treachery."

Why is he saying this? "I have no idea what you're talking about."

"You know you betrayed me." He glares down at me.

"I did no such thing, so your accusations are as absurd as you are."

"I've expected nothing more from you. How can you look at yourself in the mirror?"

"You're the one who betrayed me when I waited for your return and when our daughter was born. But, now I understand everything. I was just one of your bitches, a toy to play with. Did you use Gerda for the same purpose? The way I saw you kissing her left me with no illusions. You're good at using people. It's no surprise to learn that the only things you can offer a woman are cold diamonds and careless sex." I say it all in one gulp, open the door and dash inside. I still hear him say:

"What did you just say?" with a definite catch in his voice.

32
Finn

July 10, 1949

I HAVE A DAUGHTER. That incredible fact dances in my mind, keeping me awake all night. But I don't even know her name. I don't know anything about her. I have to find a way to talk to Wanda. She had better speak to me, or I will make her life hell. She's angry with me, and I can't comprehend why. How can she accuse me of rejecting my daughter when I didn't even know of her existence until now? Why is she blaming me for not returning to her after the war, when she was the one who betrayed and abandoned me? I'm furious with her and now set on making her pay for it. For the last five years, my heart has been dead because she betrayed me for the sake of vengeance.

I have to find a way to talk to her alone, and I know just the person to help me. Louise is a good woman, and I've known her since I moved to the States with my mother. I'm not crazy about her husband, Tony, who strikes me as a shady type of guy who thrives on Louise's money. Still, she is trustworthy, and more important, she isn't a gossip.

I enter the grand lobby of Montauk Manor, with high, wood-beam ceilings, multiple fireplaces, and stone flooring. I remember the place from before the war and always liked it for its English castle architecture. Its ballrooms were always filled with the rich and famous.

Before I even have a chance to approach the desk clerk, I hear Louise's laugh. She's on her way back from the tennis court along with a group of other women. I find out from her that Wanda decided to spend the day alone exploring the lighthouse and nearby beach while her fiancé plays golf at the Downs Golf Course. So far, I'm in luck.

I know the lighthouse is still closed to tourists, so I make my way down the steep, narrow trail near it and walk along the rocky shoreline, inhaling the salty sea air. My ears are attuned to the sound of crashing waves, while my skin enjoys the touch of warmth and a gentle breeze. Far from the hill, the lighthouse's towering cylindrical structure seems to guide me. The beach is empty.

I spot her sitting on top of a large rock, gazing out across the ocean. She looks breathtaking in a light blue summer dress. I fell in love with a gaunt girl in a tattered overcoat, so seeing her now in blooming feminine beauty takes my breath away. She will probably throw a rock at me.

I have to play this right. I want my daughter in my life. If that guy she's engaged to hangs out with Tony, that means he's not any better. Tony lives on Louise's money and social status, but the fiancé is after something else, obviously. Wanda isn't rich. This morning I called Ryan, my ex-FBI partner, and asked him to do a search on this shady guy. He's probably as devious as Wanda and even more dangerous. My stomach feels rock-hard just at the thought of it.

I inch toward her and say, "Hi."

A tan straw hat slips from her hand as she twists her body

and stares at me. In an instant, fury replaces the dreamy look on her face. She is probably dreaming about the goatee guy.

"Go away," she says and turns her face back to the ocean.

The finality of her harsh words echoes in the fizz of foam from the crashing waves. My body tenses. My mind sharpens with anger. I get straight to the point, determined to speak from my heart. That's something she did many times with me, except back then, I believed her. I just didn't suspect she was so treacherous. "Why did you do it? Why did you betray me like that?"

Her ocean-blue eyes hold a puzzled look. "What do you mean, betray you? You're the one who betrayed me."

"You broke my heart when you disappeared, leaving behind only a note that you didn't love me, and you told Veicht and Gerda my identity."

She stands up and meets my eyes with a frosty stare. "Gerda forced me to write that note. I came back the next morning to explain it to you and found the two of you in a long, passionate kiss. I saw Gerda was moving in with you." She turns her gaze toward the ocean as her tears begin to fall. "So don't tell me about your broken heart, bastard."

I clear my throat. "I had to pretend for the good of the mission and to protect my identity. You know very well I never felt anything for Gerda, besides disgust."

"Then why couldn't you just believe in my innocence and have faith in me?" Disappointment resonates in her voice.

"I saw you that day in the Café Anna with Veicht and how he kissed your hand and you happily toasted to the Third Reich."

"I can't believe this," she says shaking her head. "Anna asked me to entertain that man while she warned the uprising boys about him. I had to pretend."

"How else could Gerda have found out about me?" I direct the question as much to myself as to Wanda.

"Not from me," she says, her voice curt. "And at the time, I had no idea that Veicht was Gerda's father. Anna told me afterward because she didn't want me to panic."

I feel hollowed out. "I'm so sorry," I tell her. "I thought it was your revenge for Stefan killing your father, and that note was in your handwriting..."

"It's obvious Gerda didn't tell Veicht about you as she hoped you would marry her." Her eyes follow a seagull darting overhead, as if she needs time to compose herself, but then she focuses on me again. "Can you believe I made you blueberry pierogi that day?" She lets out an exasperated laugh. "Gerda showed up from nowhere. No time for me to hide. She must have had a key." She brushes a strand of hair away from her face. "And I must have been deep in thought since I never heard a car engine."

My heart fills with emotion. "Please, I believe you. You don't—"

She squeezes my arm. Her gentle touch electrifies my senses, burns my insides. "No, let me tell you everything."

I nod.

"Let's take a walk. It's so peaceful here."

We walk side by side along the shoreline strewn with rocks, slabs of seaweed, and shells. The salty taste of the air lingers in my mouth as I wait for her to break the silence.

"Gerda was clear that if I didn't disappear from your life, her father would go after you. She knew your true identity, and she intended to either go back to Berlin and marry you or kill you." She bends to pick up a small shell and presses it to her ear. "She gave me fifteen minutes before she intended to call the Gestapo. I thought I was doing the right thing by leaving, but I knew I would come back, and I did." She stops and tugs at her ear. "Is it okay if we walk the other way? I like the view of the lighthouse." Her eyes have begun to sparkle.

"Sure. I admire the view myself," I say.

"I kept telling myself that after the war, you would find me, so I waited. Kalina was born on April twenty-first in Tosaki, where we stayed until the end of summer before returning home. Shortly after, I started working as a translator for the American Consulate, where my fiancé, Paul, works. He helped me locate your address in New York and send a letter to you. I was happy to learn you had survived the war, and I thought you would want to know about Kalina." She glances at me. "I never heard back from you."

I clear my throat. "I never received any letters." I pause, touching her arm and finding her eyes. "I had no idea that we have a daughter. Please believe me."

She studies my face for a moment longer. "I believe you, but how can that be possible? Paul assured me that the address was correct and that he made sure it was delivered to you."

It takes a lot of effort not to curse her fiancé. "When did you start dating him?"

"Almost a year ago." She turns her face away and stares at the distant view of the lighthouse.

There's no point in wasting my energy on the goatee guy. "Tell me about her. The only thing I know is her name and age."

"She is the sweetest creature in the world. She brightens our days, and I miss her so much. My mother and Kubuś adore her." She lifts her chin. "Remember I told you about the little boy we saved?"

I nod.

"She knows that you are her daddy. She has your picture near her bed. Zuzanna gave me the film she'd found on her camera. You remember the camera her daughters had left behind, that we used to take pictures of us?"

"I do remember that." A lump comes into my throat. "Thank you for telling her about me," I say, my heart so full of love and gratitude that I think it might explode.

"I didn't want to make my parents' mistake, so I made sure our daughter would recognize you when she sees you."

"Why is she not here with you?"

A look of sadness flashes across her face. "Paul thought she would be safer at home. Five more days of torture for me." She emits a nervous laugh and glances at her watch. "I told the hotel driver to come and collect me at two o'clock, and I'm already late, so I'd better leave now." She points out the steep trail.

I bend down on my knees and look up into her eyes. "I beg you for forgiveness. I should never have doubted you in the first place. Please, forgive me. I want you and Kalina in my life. I will do everything to win you back."

For a few moments, she stares at the ocean as if I'm not even here.

"Come over tomorrow at noon to my summer house where we can talk without any interruption. My mother and grandpa are away on a cruise, so we'll be able to talk in private." I try to sound neutral, not wanting to scare her away. "Pearson's Estate, on East Lake Drive."

She twists the ring on her finger and whirls around. "Bye," she says and bolts away.

Soon she vanishes entirely from my view as a cold hand of fear of not seeing her again clutches at my heart.

33

Gerda

10 July 1949

Dear Papa,

I'm pleased to inform you that so far everything has gone according to our brilliant plan. In fact, things are turning out even better than I had expected.

Of course, that idiot is enjoying his vacation staying in this enormous summer house that looks like a fairytale castle. Yes, Papa— a castle, and I will take it even if it's on this miserable, godforsaken island. We have been living like paupers while this bastard enjoys his luxuries. But that, I assure you, will change very soon, and he will pay for what he has done to all of us, especially to me.

Anyway, I'm sure you remember the ugly portraitist I told you about, the one that he cheated with. Guess what, Papa—she is here, too. What are the odds, right? Well, it looks like I will cook two bunnies in one fire. He will watch that whore dying slowly from unbearable tortures. We will keep them alive only until we get the

information we need from him, and then it will be their fate to be
slaughtered.

We have been waiting so long for revenge, and I wish you were
here with me to enjoy every second of it.

Please, Papa, make sure to burn this letter and don't write back. I
will contact you once everything is ready for you to join us in the
luxuries of America. For now, make sure to take good care of your
health. Your recent heart attack frightened me.

Stay well,

Gerda

GERDA HAD ALWAYS FOUND it easy to write to her father. She just had to use nasty words and express how she hated their victim. Yes, Finn had become their victim the moment her father discovered his scheme. And it all happened when they received a phone call from Stefan, who had been moved to a prison in Berlin. He told her father his plans in regards to his brother.

Her father had been lucky to get a short sentence, and because of his health issues, they released him from prison after three years. Then, the planning for revenge began. Gerda couldn't wait for Stefan to join them. She wanted to rediscover the man who had been taken from her in such a twisted way. Finn didn't want her, but she hoped Stefan did.

They had been in contact for years while Stefan remained in prison. That didn't stop her dad from contacting the right people with connections and arranging Stefan's early release. Then their trip to America. Her Papa was too ill to go, so she and Stefan went. It was a long, exhausting trip, leading them to enter America illegally across the Mexican border. Still, it all turned out to be successful.

The day Stefan was released from prison was the happiest of her life, or at least that's what she first thought. Soon enough, she discovered Stefan didn't seem to care much about her. He had no passion in him and no feelings for her, and she sensed it all the way through. The only time there was a spark in his cold eyes was when they planned their trip and their revenge. He reminded her so much of her father—the same cold, calculating mind. She kept telling herself that's what she needed.

Why then does she feel disappointed in him? She shares his anger toward his brother, but that seems to be their only connection. The truth hits her hard—Stefan is incapable of loving anyone.

As angry and vindictive as Gerda is, she still wants to be loved. It's something she never got from her father or Finn, and now she can't get it from Stefan. Her mother was the only one who loved her, but she has been gone a long time now.

Gerda has already made clever decisions about her future. After they fulfill their plans, she will dupe Stefan. Now that she is older and wiser, she can decide for herself. She deserves more than what she can get from Stefan, just as her mother deserved more than what she received from her father. Gerda doesn't want to end up like her mother. Gerda is smart enough to know Stefan would never treat her right. She is sure Finn would, but he doesn't love her.

The door swings wide open. Stefan charges into their tiny room, and without a word, he collapses next to Gerda on the bed. They are staying in an obscure motel in a not so nice district of the city. Gerda doesn't even remember its name, but she knows they're still in New York City.

He turns his head to her, and their eyes meet. His stare intimidates her to the point of fear.

"We're going back to Montauk tomorrow," he says. His breath reeks of spirits. "What do you have here?" He grabs the letter from her hand.

"Give it back," she says.

"You shouldn't be sending him anything. The old fool will

let it in the wrong hands and blow our cover." He shreds Gerda's letter into pieces and drops it onto the cheap carpet.

Gerda forms her hands into fists. "He wasn't a fool back when you worked under him," she says through her clenched teeth.

His eerie laugh makes her afraid of him again.

"He let my brother fool him all the way through." He pauses and brushes his fingers off Gerda's hair. "You probably don't even know he ordered your mother's death."

Gerda's body stiffens. "It's a lie."

He gives a gruff laugh. "What a pair you both are. You gave her into the hands of the Gestapo, and he ordered her destruction. I witnessed his phone conversation with a commandant of Ravensbrück. He also asked him to send a telegram informing you of her death by typhus, just to make things easier for you."

Pain spreads through Gerda like a fire while tears burn her cheeks. "Why are you telling me this now?"

"Because I want you to stop trusting this fool. He will be dead in less than a year anyway. Look at his last heart attack, and he still drinks like a maniac." He yawns. "You belong to me now." His voice is low. "I'm the only one you have left."

Gerda is resigned to this for now. She has no one to turn to, no other place to stay, and her father approves of Stefan's treatment of her. He himself hadn't treated Gerda's mother any better.

At that moment, Gerda doesn't hate her father so much as pity him. Her blind vision of him disappeared a long time ago. At this very moment, she detests Stefan. She knows that the only way to free herself from the parasite is to kill him.

34

Wanda

July 11, 1949

THE MONTAUK MANOR'S breakfast room smells of freshly
brewed coffee and a mix of scrambled eggs and bacon. I savor
the bittersweet taste of my black coffee, loving its aromatic
scent. It's the real thing. I'm not hungry, but I work on this oat
cereal called Cheerios that I favor for its lightness and purity.
It's so much fun discovering different tastes in this foreign
country.

Much to my relief, there are only unfamiliar faces of guests
filling the tables with conversations. Paul has already left for
hunting. Before he did, he informed me in a cool voice that he
wouldn't be back until the late evening as he also plans to stop
at Downs Golf Course. I don't mind it at all, especially after last
night's conversation.

I eye the white line around my finger, which is now ringless.
It never belonged there in the first place. I knew it from the
moment I put it on. When Paul proposed, I was honest about

my feelings, declaring only friendship toward him. He insisted that the deeper feelings would come later once we were sharing our future. Now the ring is gone, put away with Paul's belongings, and I have no doubts about the rightness of it.

This trip has been an eye-opener to our relationship from the very beginning. Back home, we were coworkers at the consulate, so it was convenient to share our passion for art during our time free from work, and I liked that arrangement. But here, it feels different. I'm on vacation in a foreign country, and my fiancé spends the least possible amount of time with me. Strangely enough, it doesn't bother me a bit. It just confirms the correctness of my decision. Meeting Finn only pushed me forward with my growing desire to leave Paul.

"You don't have the decency to at least wait until when we're back home before breaking up with me," Paul said last night. A look of violence flashed over his face. "You have no idea what I had to go through to get you approved for a visa."

"I already thanked you for it so many times, Paul, but you keep bringing it up."

A flash of temper lit his eyes. "I won't even mention how much this trip has cost me."

"Well, since I paid for my ticket and contributed to the hotel bill, I feel no guilt about it. Maybe you should spend less time hunting and playing golf. If you had spent half of that time with me, maybe I wouldn't be feeling so sure about breaking up with you." I made certain there was a tone of finality in my voice.

He gave me an incredulous stare. "I thought you were having a good time with Louise?"

"Forget it." I sighed. "There's something else I need to talk to you about." I met his eyes without blinking. "I have reasons to believe that you deliberately kept my letter to Finn. You never sent it to him."

Color inflamed his cheeks. "I don't know what you're talking about," he said, taking a step back.

"You assured me that you sent my letter to Finn. I spoke with him today, and he says he never received it."

"What do you mean, you spoke with him?" He frowned.

"Why did you do it, Paul?" My stare must have been dreadful because he turned his back on me.

"He doesn't deserve you. He abandoned you, and I tried to protect you. But I don't care anymore because I know you don't love me, and you never would."

He stormed out of the hotel room and wasn't back until late at night, but the moment he hit the bed, I heard his snoring. I was able to breathe again.

After breakfast, I return to the hotel room unable to take my mind away from Finn. Tomorrow will be the last day of my stay here, and soon I'll fly back home, so I might not see him anymore.

Maybe Finn just wants to use me to find his way into Kalina's life. Judging by the way he behaved yesterday at the beach, however, it doesn't sound like it. There was honesty in his every word and depth in his gaze. Every time he touched me, strong currents of warmth and excitement ran through my body, making me want to walk into his embrace and stay there forever. The fact that he never received my letter and hadn't known about Kalina, brings me a feeling of relief.

But can the man who once doubted me be capable of the kind of love that is stable in good times and blooms in hardship? I love him in a way that I can't describe with ordinary words, as I find in him something that has always been missing within myself. I'm not convinced, though, of the depth of his feelings.

I place on the bed the summer dresses I had purchased in New York City. Between these, the cocktail dress, a bathing suit, and other accessories, I spent half of my money. However, it was all worth it because it allowed me to fit in with the other women, something impossible to achieve with my Polish outfits. Louise has invited me to spend a day tanning in the sun at the Cabana Club, so I opt for a one-piece bathing suit. For now, I plan to wear it underneath a half-sleeved, silky dress with an elastic waist and a layered, calf-length petticoat skirt. Both pieces of clothing are sunny yellow, and that color brings back memories of the night when Finn invited me to his balcony for a drink. Something pulled me to him then, and that something is doing it again.

He is on the same island, I guess only a couple of kilometers away. Maybe he spent the night with that tall brunette from the party, and perhaps right now, he doesn't even remember that he invited me over for lunch. Many things connected us back in Warsaw—all the hardship we went through. Over there, we ran on adrenalin and never-ending fear, but here, it's different—it's his home, and I'm a foreigner. He is handsome and appears to be a wealthy man, and I'm sure many women are after him. I only remind him of the dark war times, yet I'm the bearer of a new meaning in his life—the existence of our daughter.

I sense his eagerness to get to know Kalina, but he must realize her home is with me, in Poland, and he will need to adjust his life to get to know her.

Just when I've put on my bathing suit, a door knock snaps me out of my thoughts. It must be Louise. I'm already ten minutes late. When I crack it open, ready to apologize, my mouth tenses at the sight of Finn. He slides his eyes up and down my body, then grins.

"Stunning," he says in a quiet, sensual voice.

My cheeks grow warm. "I was expecting Louise," I say, averting my eyes. If I take one more dive into his intense gaze, I won't be able to stop myself from leaping into his embrace. Everything inside me is already melting just from the way he watches me. So instead, I stare at his casual, crisp white shirt that so admirably complements his muscular body.

"I just spoke to her, and she asked me to tell you she isn't feeling well today and has to cancel your plans at the Cabana Club." He smiles down at me with sheer satisfaction, his teeth gleaming against his sun-tanned skin. "Migraines can be rough."

I wonder if there is any part of my body that isn't right now burning red. Yesterday he invited me over for lunch, but instead, I made plans with Louise. "Oh, poor Louise, I hope she feels better. If you will excuse me now—"

He places his hand between the door and the frame. "My offer for lunch still stands, especially now that your plans have been canceled."

When I don't answer right away, he glances at my hand, now with a missing ring. "I already prepared it. I worked so hard on those lamb sandwiches, so please don't turn me down." His voice is filled with pleading, his eyes with longing.

"I don't favor lamb, but I feel bad for all the effort you've put in," I say, treating him to the most grateful smile I could muster. "Just let me change."

"If you ask me, your attire is perfect," he says, letting his gaze wander down my body.

This man drives me crazy. "I'll meet you downstairs in ten minutes," I say, closing the door on him.

* * *

Driving in Finn's maroon Lincoln convertible coupe is quite a challenging experience because of the wind smacking my face and messing with my hair. I curse myself for forgetting my hat. When we approach a narrow dirt road, Finn cruises his vehicle at a lower speed. Clouds of dust make me choke, but soon enough we park in front of a miniature, white fairytale castle with a rubble-stone turreted tower. I catch myself gaping at this gorgeous home.

He switches off the engine. "Hope the ride wasn't too rough on you?" His note of concern is genuine.

I can't help but laugh. "Even with a ruined hairdo and dust between my teeth, I still think this ride is a pleasure compared to when you drove me to my home in Żoliborz when the speakers blasted out. I was so terrified of your reaction."

He smiles. "I was too busy wondering why my performance at Café Anna had brought you to such a desperate act of gulping down half a bottle of vodka." He ruffles my hair playfully. "Now, I'm about to prove that I'm much better at cooking than singing." He winks, lifts my ringless hand, and kisses it. He has a meaningful look in his eyes.

I ignore my pounding heart. "You have a beautiful summer home."

He nods. "The entire credit goes to my Grandpa. He built it in the late twenties and rebuilt it again after the 1938 hurricane. He has a soft spot for Montauk."

"He seems as determined as you are," I say.

A brief laugh emanates from him. "I have a surprise for you."

He asks me to wait for him while he disappears into the *castle*, only to reappear a minute later with a wooden basket filled with food and a blanket over his arm. "I thought it would be nice to have a picnic on the beach," he says, an earnest look on his face.

A feeling of excitement flutters deep in the pit of my stomach. "That sounds wonderful."

His face lights up. "Just so you know, that's not the only surprise I have in store for you." He kisses my hand.

We take a narrow, steep path to the beach. I inhale the salty sea air with pleasure.

"I could live on the beach, if you ask me," I say while we walk in search of a picnic spot. The only visible people are out in the far distance.

He laughs at the very idea. "I thought so. What about here?" He points to an empty spot near a large rock, not far from the shore.

I nod and take off my sandals, digging my toes into the hot sand to reach the bottom layer that cools and massages my feet. The sky is clear and wide, and the breeze is gentle on my skin.

"It's heaven," I say, watching Finn spreading the blanket on the sand. "Do you need my help?"

"I have it all under control. I want you to enjoy being here." He gestures toward the ocean.

So I do. I face the ocean with my ears tuned to the crash of waves and the fizz of foam as it sweeps ashore and to the sounds of crying seagulls looking for food. I can't get enough of it.

"Time for some exquisite food." Finn's teasing voice comes from behind me.

His lamb sandwiches on white bread taste so good. "This is delicious. I thought I didn't like lamb, but I guess when you make it, it does taste good."

He winks. "I told you I'm an excellent cook."

We chat about silly things and drink red wine that is smooth and rich. I like the hint of berries in it, though it is not as good as Mrs. Kowalska's sweet wine.

When we finish, he insists I relax while he gathers the leftovers and places them in the basket.

"Would you like to go for a walk?" he asks, his lazy gaze on me.

It relaxes me so much to be here with him that I forget my worries about my family back in Poland. But then, I know it won't last much longer, and in a couple of days, I will be leaving for home. I feel torn between the wonderful thought of returning to my family and the painful realization of separating from Finn once more. I want him back in my life.

"I'd like that," I say. "Maybe you can tell me more about the lighthouse."

"Sure."

I raise myself off the blanket and extend my hand to him.

He takes it and pulls me into his strong embrace. My insides melt when his burning lips brush my earlobe, then move to the nape of my neck and my lower lip. I can't gather the strength to turn my head away. His mouth becomes insistent, demanding my response, and when I succumb, the kiss becomes pure, tormenting sensuality. Engrossed in the flames of his masculine strength, I want this moment to go on forever. There is no other man in this universe who can make me feel that way. Only Finn Keller.

A few minutes later, we are walking along the shore holding our hands.

"Let's go in the water," he says, tugging my hand.

"I can't swim, and I don't have a baiting suit."

"I can teach you." He takes his shirt off and then grins at me. "And no suits required."

"What are you doing?" I ask and smile in disbelief as he strips and runs toward the water. I blush and look around, but to my relief, there is no one in sight. I'm seeing a new side of Finn.

He spreads out his arms, tilts his head back, and calls out, "I love Wanda." He repeats it a few times and then shoots me an earnest look. "Come to me."

My heart melts. "You are crazy," I say, unable to suppress my laugh. But I love watching his spontaneous act of happiness. I never saw him that way back in Poland because there were always so many worries and dangers. Here everything seems so simple.

"If you don't get your cute butt down here, I may decide to vanish in the current," he says. "At this point, it's up to you to save my pride."

"You're mad." I'm not sure if he hears me, as my voice is lost in a crush of waves. And then, to my terror, he isn't in view anymore. I stop breathing, waiting for him to reappear, but there is nothing.

I swallow hard. Why is he doing this to me? I know he's just faking to make me join him. I resist another minute before a rush of adrenaline surges through me.

"Finn, stop this!" When there is no response, I move forward. Now I'm in water up to my chest, but he's still not in sight. "Finn!"

To my utter relief, I feel his hands around my waist, and he reappears right in front of me.

"You came," he says beaming.

I put my hands on his chest and try to push him away. "That wasn't funny." I glare at him. "I thought something happened to you, and I knew I couldn't help you." I can feel tears of frustration forming, so I turn away from him. "I told you I can't swim."

He pulls me back to him. "I'm sorry." He lifts my chin. "I acted like a fool. Please forgive me."

I don't have the heart to be upset with him any longer. I should have known he was just pretending. "No, I just overreacted. I'm embarrassed." I smile, unable to meet his eyes.

"It was cute, and I loved it." He smirks. "Can we do it again?"

"Stop tormenting me," I say, still avoiding his gaze.

"Look at me." His voice is quiet but serious.

When I do, his gentle smile captivates me. This man is far from making fun of me. "The reason I enjoyed your reaction so much is that it's amazing to know you do care. I spent all those years thinking the only feeling you ever had for me was hatred, and you wanted my blood just like my brother. It hurt to no end to wake up every day and be reminded of it. Not a day went by when I didn't think of you and miss you.

"I hated myself for it, but I couldn't help it. When I first saw you that evening at the Island Club, I wanted so badly to despise you, and I convinced myself that meeting you again could ultimately free me from you. But when I saw you with Paul, I couldn't help but feel jealous."

"I never stopped loving you, not even when I believed you rejected Kalina," I whisper and kiss him on the mouth. I sense his shock at first, but soon he deepens the kiss, and I feel a blissful warmth taking over every part of me.

"Let's leave," he says in a husky voice. "You don't want to know what I want to do to you right now."

* * *

The next day I meet with Finn at the beach near the lighthouse. He promised to show it to me, even though it's closed to the public. It turns out he knows the keeper, and soon we are climbing the stairs up to the tower.

"This view is breathtaking," I say, unable to contain my awe at the sweeping sight of the endless ocean.

"So I take it you are not afraid of heights at all." He stands behind me, his hands around my waist.

I lean back and rest my head on his chest. "I'm kind of afraid, but your company makes me feel safe."

He laughs. "I wouldn't be much help if you decided to jump, so please just do me a favor and stay still."

I turn back to him and find his gaze. "You still make me feel safe." I'm not talking about the tower, and he knows it because his face grows serious.

He holds up my chin. "I won't disappoint you this time." We embrace, and his kiss leaves me lightheaded.

"Have dinner with me tonight," he whispers.

"You're such a charmer."

"Does that mean *yes*?"

I love the pleading look on his face, and I want nothing more than to spend as much time as possible with him before going back home. "Only if you promise to leave the cooking to me." I chuckle.

"I see. You don't trust my cooking abilities." He tilts his head back and gives a long, heartwarming laugh.

An hour later, before we step over the threshold of his *castle*, Finn lifts me off the ground and into his arms.

I laugh at his ridiculous gesture. "You are so silly, Finn. I'm not your bride," I say. "Put me down."

But there is no sign of humor on his face. He kicks the door behind us and shuts it with his foot. "What I feel for you is beyond any rules," he says, his eyes blazing into mine. "Being with you means home to me. I won't let you leave this time."

My breath catches. I cup his face in my hands. "You truly mean it?"

"You need proof to believe?" He grins.

The soft touch of his skin and the familiar woodsy scent of his cologne make every inch of me crave him.

"I won't put you down until you believe me." He lifts my chin and plants his sensual lips on my mouth. His kiss is thrilling and demanding, and when his tongue finds mine, the kiss deepens, releasing depths of pleasure stored in me for all those years apart.

My heart beats fast from a combination of longing and excitement. No other man could make me feel the way Finn's touch does, as if he knows every tender point in my body. When he lifts his mouth, I smile and say, "I'm still not convinced."

He laughs deep in his throat. "I haven't even started yet, so you must be patient." He puts me down and reaches into his pocket to retrieve a small, square box.

He bends to his knee, extends his hand toward me, and opens the box to reveal a gorgeous ring centered with a heart-shaped diamond.

My heart skips in confusion as I stare, first at the ring and then into his deep eyes.

"*Kochanie*, darling, I know you don't care for diamonds, but this one is special and can only belong to you. Before my Grandma passed, she gave it to me, making me promise to find the woman I truly love. I know you are engaged, or maybe not anymore..." He gazes at my ringless hand. "But I fell in love with you the moment I laid eyes on you, and my feelings have only deepened since then. The years without you have been so numb and empty, and it's only now that I feel alive again." He takes the ring out of the box and melts his gaze into mine. "Will you marry me?"

Joy overwhelms me. I feel my tears emerging and don't try to stop them. I want to say yes, but that one word is stuck in my throat.

With a heartfelt look on his face, he says, "You don't have to answer now. I can wait."

"Yes." I finally let that one word burst out and I smile with delight.

Joy fills his face like sunshine. He slips the ring on my finger, and then he kisses me with such intensity that I feel his longing in every fiber of my body.

While he walks up the stairs, holding me in his arms, I bury my face in the warmth of his arm. If this man wants me even half as much as I want him, we are in for big trouble.

* * *

Lying in bed in Finn's embrace feels fresh and crisp, like inhaling a briny sea air. The delicious touch of his muscular body makes me feel drunk, spent from endless hours of lovemaking. Butterflies tickle at my stomach at the thought of Finn's gentle, sensual touch. The way he caresses and teases my body gives me limitless pleasure and leaves me in a state of bliss. I wonder if such intensity is even possible; it seems more like one of my dreams. Maybe the one true love has to be like that. So powerful, but then able to be abandoned because someone decided to play with our lives, to ruin them. Finn didn't come back after the war because the false belief that I had betrayed him hurt to no end.

"What are you thinking about, darling?" he asks, caressing my cheek with his palm.

"I'm wondering if it's even possible to love with such intensity."

"We are proof that it is," he whispers. "Without you, I'm just a lost, incomplete fool, and I won't let you leave me again."

"So this is why you lured me to your bed, so I don't leave?" I lift my head from his chest to gaze at him, allowing my lips to quirk. "I wonder if you even made those lamb sandwiches the other day."

He laughs lazily. "Guilty on both counts. My housekeeper made them."

"Why do I know you so well?"

He grins, but instead of answering me, he engages us in a long, heart-stealing kiss. When he lifts his mouth, I feel dazed.

"Let me go grab something to drink, princess." He runs his hand through my hair and climbs off the bed.

I snuggle my face into the pillow, unable to contain my grin, my happiness. Yes, the absolute heaven of being with the man I wanted so badly for so long. I need to pinch my cheek just to confirm all of this isn't merely a dream.

It feels lovely to drink wine and laugh together.

"Tell me about your family in Poland," he says.

"We still live with my mother in our old house in Żoliborz. We grew to care for Kubuś so much that I decided to adopt him. He is such a good boy and an amazing brother to Kalina."

"I'm sure your father is at peace looking at all of you."

I take a sip of wine and sigh. "I hope so. I have been lucky so far to be left alone by the Soviet-driven system that we have in Poland now. I think it's because of my involvement with the American Consulate." I sigh and put down my glass. "Many people are being interrogated. People like my brother and myself are declared traitors and given death sentences. Anna convinced Mateusz to flee to England, where they got married. He works in a hospital in London as a pediatrician. They named their son after Tata. Have you kept in touch with Zuzanna? She lives in Canada with her daughter now."

"Nope, but Ignacy wrote that she moved there with the children." There's a faint catch in his voice.

"You know Witek was killed in the uprising, right?"

"Yes." We stay silent for a moment. "I always wondered what happened to the rickshaw boy with freckles."

"He survived. Now he studies geology at Warsaw University." I smile. "He is still the same, shy, but I know there are many girls who have a crush on him."

He grins. "His personality is different from Manfred's, but still, he somehow reminded me of him."

"What happened to Manfred?"

"He is still my assistant." He laughs contentedly. "He works at my Grandpa's law firm in Manhattan. Well, now *my* firm."

"You continued in law school?" I give him a dazed look.

"Not right away. At first, I worked as an FBI agent, but then Grandpa threatened to disinherit me if I didn't go back to school and take over his business. Same pressure came from my mother."

"I wonder if they are even going to like me," I say. I imagine their surprise when they learn Finn has a daughter. Will they judge me? It's hard for me to believe they will welcome us with open arms.

He puts his glass down, moves the tray from the bed to the nightstand, and pulls me into his arms. "They will, and if not, I will always choose you and Kalina. You have nothing to worry about." He kisses my forehead. "Have you connected with your biological mother's side of the family?"

"My grandparents died during the uprising. Their tenement collapsed while they were in the basement. My mother was their only child, and I couldn't find any other relatives." I sigh. "I will never get to learn much about her."

"At least you have that picture," he says.

"I do, and I'm so thankful, at least for that." After a long silence, I say, "I may just stay in the Montauk Manor for the rest of my trip. It's nicer here than in the city with my ex-fiancé."

"Wait, so you already broke up with him?"

"Yes."

He engages me with another kiss. "I'll help you move your things here. It's your home now."

"Are you sure?"

"Absolutely. I have to drive to the city in the morning to

take care of some things in the office, but I will be gone only for a couple of hours. Will you be fine?"

"Of course." I give him a playful look. "I will finally get a chance to relax at the beach, since you have been so persistent in distracting me."

35
Finn

"THE GUY IS CLEAN," my red-haired, Herculean-built friend Ryan says, referring to Wanda's ex-fiancé, Paul. He has called my office line, and, after a friendly chat, mainly about his two-week vacation in Ireland, he cuts to the reason for his call. "He stays out of trouble."

"Just needed to make sure. Thanks, brother," I say. I'm not concerned about the guy anymore, not after Wanda agreed to marry me.

"Have you had another anonymous letter?" he asks. After so many missions as FBI agents, we know each other well, and I swear there is a hint of concern in his voice.

"Nope, only the one I found a couple of weeks ago. Maybe it was just a joke—you know—there are a quite few angry women after me."

"That's an understatement." He lets out a gruff laugh. "Every woman in the city thinks your heart is made out of iron."

"You're damn right." I grin. "But, as of yesterday, I'm engaged."

There follows a short silence on his side. "Ha, ha. Funny. You got me this time."

"To Wanda." At the thought of our engagement, my heart is beating with relief.

"Wanda? Like Wanda from Poland? You've got to be kidding me. I thought you hated her."

"I was such a fool. It's a long story. I'll tell you when we get together."

"Sure, my friend. I'm so happy for you," he says, laughter in his voice. "I assume she is there with you?"

"In Montauk. But our daughter is still in Poland."

"Wait. Did you say, *daughter*?"

I lean back in my chair. "I know this all sounds crazy."

"Yup, definitely too long for a phone conversation. I'm coming over this weekend, so we can catch up then, and you can tell me all."

"Let's plan fishing off Montauk, like last time."

"I'm in. Listen, so you said no more anonymous notes, right?" His voice throbs again.

"Right." He has something important to tell me.

"Good. You might be right that it's nothing to worry about then, and there's just some crazy woman after you."

"What is it that you're not telling me, my friend?"

"When was the last time you were in contact with your brother?" His voice is quiet and tense.

I clear my throat. "You know I haven't seen him since the end of the war," I say. After visiting him in prison in London, I never found the heart in me to contact him again. I had been hiding most of his terrible deeds from our mother—the truth would have killed her. She sent him packages regularly and even visited a couple of times. Still, she came back home every time with a broken heart because that bastard refused to even see her. Since I told Grandpa the truth, he made a point never to mention Stefan again.

"When you told me about the anonymous letter, I decided to do a check on him. Guess what I just learned?"

After a short silence, he continues, "He's out of prison."

I grip the arm of my chair. "How's that even possible? He was sentenced to twenty-five years."

"I only found this out today, so I don't know any details besides the fact that he left on June 13. Don't worry, I'll dig into it and call you the moment I know more." Assurance fills his voice. "Come on, you have nothing to worry about. He definitely won't be able to leave Germany for a very long time."

I pound my fist on the table. "What a miserable world. It's unthinkable that after what they've done, they get away with only a few years in prison." I say, my voice suddenly empty.

"I feel your pain, brother. But it's not over yet. There are still pending trials. And as to your brother, I already have people working on it. I have your butt covered."

I don't share Ryan's optimism. If Stefan is out, he will come after me, sooner or later. I'm sure of it, but I need to wait until Ryan finds out more before taking any action, and he does his job right. He's one of the best agents out there, and I'm lucky to have his help. Still, a sense of danger gnaws at my stomach. Something is off. "Can you check if he has crossed the border?"

"Jimmy is working on it as we speak. Don't worry, man. He's on it."

"Yes, Jimmy is the best." An image of Jim's cheerful face surrounded by his curly haircut brings a smile. "Thanks, big guy. I truly appreciate it."

"Don't mention it. Are you both staying at your summer house?"

"Yes."

"Okay. I'll call you there when I hear from Jimmy. I have to go now but talk to you soon. Try staying out of trouble."

"You bet."

It isn't only for myself I fear—I now have a family to protect. My brother is a vicious beast who wants my blood. Someone has to be helping him, someone outside of prison. Gerda Veicht? I need to protect Wanda and Kalina, and there is only one way to accomplish it. I need to go to Germany before Stefan comes here—or worse before he goes to Poland while I'm here.

Wanda

I SPEND most of my day at the beach. Finn's empty house awakens memories of the years spent apart, the nights filled with longing and heartache. Somehow it also reminds me of Kalina's absence, the precious little girl who saved me by capturing my heart.

I sketch the Montauk lighthouse; I memorized its every detail. I shade Abigail the Ghost into it, as I'm intrigued by the story Finn told me the other day. A captain's young wife, Abigail, was the only survivor of a ship that wrecked near the lighthouse on Christmas Day of 1811. She washed ashore but died soon after, and ever since then, her spirit has roamed the lighthouse. I envision her as an angelic girl in a white dress with flames of red curls.

I put the drawing aside and inhale the sea air with pleasure. All this is so foreign to me. When I was growing up, my parents took my brother and me on summer vacations to the Baltic Sea's crowded beaches, but here it's empty and peaceful. I watch a sailboat in the distance and think how different this world is from my home, where I live in constant terror of the

Soviet-driven system. It's so relaxing to sit on the beach and watch seagulls darting overhead or dig my feet into the warm sand. Yet, I can't wait to go back to my children and Mama. Life without them means nothing to me.

It's already late afternoon. The sunlight bathes everything in a golden glow. I walk back to the house, hoping to find Finn there, but the driveway is empty. The house smells of floor wax and freshly cut flowers. Finn mentioned that the housekeeper would come at noon to clean, but she is already gone. I move toward the curving stairway, once more admiring the high ceilings, crystal chandeliers, stone fireplace, and granite floors. The decor itself gives away Finn's mother's taste for large landscape paintings and her love of music, as a grand piano stands apart from the rest of the furniture.

After I shower and put on my white summer dress, I decide to wait for Finn upstairs. The room with a large bed in the middle and cozy rugs is nearly as big as my entire house. It feels less lonely to be in his bedroom with the scent of his cologne lingering in the air. The softness of the bedsheets brings the memory of the previous night's lovemaking.

For a second, I hear the screeching sound of the door being closed downstairs. It's strange because no other noises or footsteps follow. I climb off the bed and walk to the window. There is no car in the driveway, so it isn't Finn. A fog rolls in overhead while a gust of wind sways the trees. I sprint to the nightstand and take out the pistol Finn showed me this morning. I laughed when he did, but he had a serious expression on his face, and now it terrifies me to even think about it. Did he anticipate danger?

Bursts of rain crash against the windows—maybe it was just the wind that made the noise downstairs. Yes, it was just the wind. I need to calm down, or I will give myself another anxiety attack. I return the pistol to the drawer and resolve to go to the kitchen to prepare dinner for us, or at least check what the housekeeper left. But the second I step into the hall, something hard strikes my head. Everything turns black.

* * *

I awaken to a throbbing pain in my head and Finn's face in front of me, except those fierce eyes can't be his. My stomach churns. Stefan? He has propped me against the wooden bed frame, my hands tied behind my back, and my legs immobilized with a rope. The draperies are shut tight, and the harsh light from the ceiling lamp hurts my eyes. I can't make sense out of the situation I find myself in. I want this to be just a bad dream. I thought Finn's brother was in prison, when in fact, he deserved the death penalty. What the hell is he doing here?

"What—"

"Shut up, bitch," he says in a dangerous voice. "For your own good." His behavior doesn't match the elegant charcoal suit he's wearing.

"But—"

He smacks me in the face.

I wince and close my eyes. What a brute. The same monster that killed Tata now is hurting me. I swallow hard trying to calm myself. I must be strong and think clear. I must figure out how to warn Finn as he will be back any moment now.

"I told you to shut up. Don't worry. You'll see your lover soon enough to say goodbye." He lets out a small, derisive laugh.

"You look so handsome," says a voice at a distance. A woman in a white dress almost fills the height of the doorframe.

My pulse races. What is Gerda doing here? And then, it all becomes clear—they are here after Finn.

"I give my brother credit for good taste. This tailored suit fits me perfectly. What a change from prison scraps," Stefan says, his clean-shaven face rigid like iron. "I will also give my dear brother a classy welcome and a glimpse at how things are going to be when he is gone."

Gerda walks toward him and adjusts his tie. "You'll certainly do a better job than he does, and you deserve all of it."

"I'm so damn ready for my new life." He pulls her into an embrace.

A cynical smile twists her lips. "He might arrive any time now."

"I can't wait." They kiss for a long moment.

When he walks away, Gerda turns to me, her face wrinkled in disgust. "So sad I have to look at your ugly mouth again."

"Cut it, Gerda. I'm not going to play your nasty games."

She sneers at me. "I see the scared little girl got thicker skin on her back."

"What are you trying to pull?"

She ignores my question. "I see we have matching outfits. The tragic news is that yours will soon be stained with blood and dirt."

"You are sick." My voice sounds shaky, even to my own ears.

"I'm sure that little girl and the one-armed boy will miss you."

"Why are you telling me all of this?"

"I'm just preparing you for the inevitable. You will share your lover's fate tonight, and most likely the same grave." Her lips curl in self-appreciative amusement.

"You won't get away with it. Finn worked for the FBI, so they will investigate and put your ass in jail, just where you belong," I say, glaring at her.

"You still don't get it, do you?"

I force a laugh. "Oh, yes, Gerda, I understand your little

scheme. Do you think Finn's mother or grandfather won't recognize Stefan? Do you think they won't call the police or the FBI?"

"No worries, we'll take care of them too. I'm a genius when it comes to planning."

"That's right. You betrayed your own mother."

She jerks backward.

I hit the hot spot. "Where is she now, Gerda? Dead because of you?"

She kicks my stomach, making me yelp in pain. "Shut up, whore." Her round face reddens.

"What would she want you to do, Gerda? Would she like to see you hurting other people, just like you hurt her?"

"You don't know what you are talking about."

"I get it. It must be tough to live with the knowledge that you contributed to your mother's death."

She glares at me. "I didn't want to betray her, but I had to do what the Führer ordered. And it was for her own good, too."

"Did Hitler's *Mein Kampf* teach you such cruelty, or was it your father's influence?"

"You don't understand. No one does." Her voice softens. "My generation was the chosen one. We had expectations to fulfill."

"So you fulfilled yours by breaking the heart of your mother, who loved you beyond all words. Worse, you betrayed her and signed her death sentence." I pause, weighing my next words. "It's not too late, Gerda. You can still make her proud. You can still atone for your sins and make peace with yourself. Stefan is a sick man, and one day he will kill you, too."

For a moment, a trace of confusion crosses her face, but she recovers quickly. "My mother had a need to save others, even at the price of putting her own family at risk. I only tried to reverse her actions, to help her."

"Do you think your father would have rejected you, too, if you had followed her path, not his?"

"He would have sent me to Ravensbrück..." Her voice fades.

"Gerda, get your butt down here." Stefan's voice jerks her out of the transfixed state.

"Gerda, you can still make changes in your life," I say, unable to remove a pleading tone from my voice.

"It's too late, Wanda." She walks away.

For the first time, she has called me by my name and not by an epithet. So, there is a soft spot in Gerda, but it's hard to make it surface. She seems vulnerable at the mention of her mother, almost as if no one ever talks to her about it.

The desperate sense of powerlessness grows so intense in me that it hurts even to breathe. The thought of not seeing my children ever again gnaws at my heart. My fear for Finn, who is about to face these two dangerous lunatics, escalates. Everything is out of my control, but still, I have in me a spark of unrealistic yet stubborn hope. There was only one other time I felt the same way—during the night in Pawiak Prison five years ago. Finn proved that the impossible was possible after all, and he found a way to save me. Now it's my turn to save him, and I have to think of something before it's too late.

I pull on my hands, trying to get some slack in the rope, and find loose ends with my fingers. Then I wiggle my hands to find the knot, but the task is way too tricky. I keep on trying and listen carefully for any noises from outside, so I can scream and warn Finn before he enters the house. My plan collapses the moment Stefan returns to stuff a cloth in my mouth.

About fifteen minutes later, I hear a car pulling in. Finn. I pray he notices something unusual and doesn't come in. I hear the engine turn off. I try to make as much noise as possible, but a couple of minutes later, a rumbling noise comes from downstairs. My heart sinks.

Stefan drags Finn's limp body and, with Gerda's help, props him up on a chair about five meters across from me. He straps Finn's arms and legs to it.

"Let's have dinner," Stefan says to Gerda. "I'm sure the icebox is brimming with all sorts of delicacies." He gives a bitter laugh. "By the time we finish, the son of a bitch should be awake."

Before walking away, he switches off the light.

Soon, my eyes adjust to the darkness of the room, and I settle my gaze on Finn's lifeless figure. I take in his features as if I intend to sketch him. The last sketch of the man who means everything to me. The man I'm ready to sacrifice myself for. If only my feelings were enough to free him from his deranged brother. But I know we are both destined for the same fate.

I force my imagination to make one last sketch of my love. In my mind, I trace every inch of his body with utmost precision, like never before. And then, I concentrate on his intense eyes, warm smile, pointed nose, and high cheekbones. Every detail of him is so dear to me. By the time I complete the imaginary sketch, tears are flowing down my face. If we survive this nightmare, I vow to paint his portrait every year on his birthday.

My love for Finn isn't just about words or gestures. I feel it in every fiber of my being. But that isn't enough to save him, so I pray. I offer my heart to God, begging for a miracle.

It should be the beginning of us, not the end. He hasn't even met our daughter yet. It's so cruel for fate to erase us like unneeded lines in a pencil drawing.

Finn's head jerks up, and a painful groan emerges from his throat.

37

Gerda

WHILE STEFAN HELPS himself to food he finds in the icebox, Gerda has no appetite. She rather feels like vomiting, so she settles on the sofa in the family room, a small notebook and pencil in her hands. She's been working on her first romance novel. Writing about characters falling in love gives her a thrill of accomplishment.

But at the moment, she desperately needs to write to her Mutti.

Dear Mutti,
I'm so sorry.
I never stopped loving you.

"What the hell are you doing here, sugar?" Stefan stands in the door frame, his hands folded at his chest.

She hides the notebook behind her. "I'm not hungry."

"Well, it's time to go back up there then." He smirks.

"We should just lock them away in the basement, clear

Finn's accounts, and disappear. I'm sure he'll give you all the information just to save his mistress."

"That's not the plan, idiot," he shouts at her. "Have you lost your mind?"

She springs to her feet and meets his gaze. She's not sure why, but for the first time in a long time, she is not afraid of him. "If we kill them, we will have the authorities on our backs. It's wiser to take the money and disappear without hurting anyone."

His gaze hardens into a glare, and he says through his clenched teeth, "They will both be dead in ten minutes."

The finality in his voice snaps Gerda back to reality just as fear is crippling her again. "As you wish." She takes her pistol out and heads upstairs.

"Good girl," he says and follows her lead.

3 8

Finn

MY HEAD FEELS like someone just took a hammer to it. What the hell...

The ceiling light snaps on, hurting my vision. The moment my eyes recover and adjust to the harsh light, adrenalin shoots through my system. Someone has tied Wanda too and stuffed her mouth with a cloth. Her darting gaze locks on mine. She appears afraid but calm, as if she's trying to take strength from my eyes.

"Hope you're enjoying the show," I hear the chilling, familiar voice of my brother. He nears me and leans against the closet door, FP-45 pistol in his hand. He speaks in German.

A cold sweat films my body. "What the hell do you think you're doing, Stefan?"

"Might as well start calling me Finn," he says and grins. "It will help me to get used to it." He spreads his arms. "You have good taste, little brother. I'll keep some of your wardrobe."

"You're sick." He's here to do what he promised in every letter he had sent me. How did he manage to cross the border? Why was he released from prison?

He lets out a scoffing laugh. "You never cared to show me any respect." His face hardens. "I was always in your shadow. Now everything is about to change."

"Bullshit. You were the one who always took everyone's attention." I hear my voice getting louder and louder as I spit the words at my brother. I know he's crazy, but I must somehow convince him to spare us. "Mutter was busy running around fixing your disastrous deeds until the day when you shut her down by trying to cut her throat open. You took away all her strength, and to this day, she's just a wreck of herself."

"I wasn't the one to wreck her. I only followed the example of the big shot lawyer, our dearest Daddy." He throws his head back. "But I'm not here to discuss our childhood. I hate all of you. I'm ashamed even to be a part of this family."

"So this is why you refused to see her when she visited you in prison?" He's unable to feel guilt.

"She isn't worth my time, just like you're not." He glares at me. "You betrayed me." He moves his gaze to his pistol. "You were the only one I trusted. You always tried to understand me, and even your long speeches about morals never bothered me. I never intended to get in your way or hurt you until the day you helped those Polish bastards shut me down, and then, you took my place."

So he knows I replaced him. "You were murdering innocent people," I say. "Don't act like you're the one deserving of pity."

"You took my place and left me at the mercy of those Polish parasites. You don't deserve to be called my brother, and today, you and your whore will pay for your betrayal."

My mind sobers. My thinking sharpens. I have to find another way to get to him, to make him spare us. "You were given a death sentence by the Polish underground, and I was the one to save you. I convinced them to change the death sentence to time in prison. You're alive today because of me."

"I'm far from thanking you. Let me assure you of that." He smirks. "The cards have changed, and now you're the one with your hands tied. To your misfortune, my heart is not as kind as yours."

There's no point in arguing with him; I already learned this years ago. "If this is about money, take whatever you want. Set us free, and I'll transfer it into your name."

"I want your blood."

"Then at least let her go. She never did you any wrong." I struggle to remove the begging pitch from my voice.

"Why would I deprive myself of the joy of watching you witness her agony? Plus, our dear Gerda has been looking forward to this little entertainment. Seems like she took a terrible dislike to your mistress."

"I will give you anything you want." My voice cracks.

He gives a long, derisive laugh.

"I love you, brother. It's not too late to repair things between us. Let us go, and I will never report any of this. You don't need to pretend to be me to get money. I will transfer whatever you need to your bank account," I say.

"I'm not taking your goddamned bullshit. You did nothing to prove your love. But what is love, anyway? Just an empty, meaningless word. You mean nothing to me, and the only thing that will make me happy right now is the thought of this long-overdue revenge. I have waited for this day since the moment you betrayed me, and I intend to enjoy it."

He lifts his eyes to something behind me. "Gerda, we're done with our little chitchat. It's time to move forward," he says.

Gerda appears and moves closer to Wanda, a pistol in her hand. Her demeanor has changed; she seems quiet and somehow absent. The old Gerda would glare at me and not hesitate to hurl insults my way, as it was her greatest weapon.

"You look like you just saw a ghost? What's going on with you?" Stefan's voice boils with impatience.

"I'm fine, Stefan. Shut up."

"That's my girl." He smiles, exposing his white teeth. "Why don't you start the show, but remember to do it exactly as I told you. This whore needs to suffer a slow, painful death."

Wanda's eyes widen, and my spine stiffens at his words. "Don't do it, Gerda. You've never killed before—don't start now."

She turns my way and studies my face. Her eyes betray a hint of softness.

A spark of hope brushes at my heart. Something has changed in her through the years, and she isn't as impulsive and harsh. Why is she here with Stefan, then? "Be like your mother, Gerda. She was a good woman."

She winces, as if my words smacked her in the cheek, but she remains silent.

"Shut your mouth." Stefan presses the pistol to my forehead and cocks it.

"I can't do it." Gerda steps back from Wanda.

"What the hell?" Stefan jerks away from me and points the gun in Wanda's direction. "You are such a chicken, sugar. I'll show you right now how to handle this." He grins at Gerda. "Just watch me."

He stands close enough for me to reach him. I tense my muscles and use all my strength to force my body to move with the chair and crash into his back. The moment he crumples, I try to jerk the pistol from his grasp using my tied hands. He recovers immediately and leaps to his feet, jumping away from me.

"You are brain dead," he says, his breathing shallow. "Now you stay like that." He crushes my head with his shoe, and I think my skull is about to split in half. "You are going to lie here like a crippled parasite while I put your whore through unimaginable agony."

God, please, if you are there, please save her. I haven't prayed for years, but in this terrifying moment, you're my only hope. I close my eyes and fill my mind with the prayer Pani Ela taught me when I was little. The prayer that completely entrusts my fate into God's hands. I feel something soothing envelop my sorrow.

The sound of the pistol shot deafens my ears, freezing the blood in my veins. Tears sting my eyes. I jerk my head back to find Wanda untouched, her eyes wide open, like she's in shock. Then I realize that Stefan's foot is no longer pressing against my head. I turn my head sideways to see his lifeless body next to me. As if hypnotized, Gerda stands beside him, a gun still in her trembling hand.

My brother is gone, leaving only a metallic scent of gunpowder in his wake. He chose the dark side until the end. I lost him a long time ago, but still, I blame myself once more for being unable to save him, to convince him to act for good. I move my gaze back to Wanda. Her gentle eyes connect with mine. Tears run down her cheeks. Then I feel the thrill that God has listened to my prayers and spared her.

"I'm sorry, darling," I say, trying to stop my tears, but the damn tears don't listen.

The ordeal isn't over yet, not until Gerda drops the gun. She's riveted in the same position, staring at Stefan, the gun in her hand, pointed at him as if she's making sure he doesn't rise again.

"Are you okay, Gerda?" I ask, trying to bring her back to reality. She's the only one who can free us, but at the same time, I worry she will choose to get rid of us. I still have a picture of the old Gerda in my mind. People don't change that easily.

She moves her gaze to me. Her pale blue eyes blaze into mine, almost as if she needs my approval for what she did.

"You did the right thing. Your mother is proud of you."

"I had no choice," she says in a low, pained voice. "He was going to kill us all. He thought I was stupid." She lets out a nervous laugh and eyes her gun. "He was a cold bastard, and I hated him. I wasn't going to let him hurt me the same way my father hurt my mother."

She glances at Wanda and then comes back to me. "I fell in love with you, not him. You treated me with respect and kindness, even though I behaved like a spoiled brat.

"When Stefan came out of prison, I thought we could start over, but the only thing he cared about was revenge. I had no strength to leave my father and him, no strength to refuse to be a part of this scheme. So I made my own plan.

"At first to kill Stefan when he least expected it, and then to kill her." She points to Wanda with her pistol. "So I can have you, the only man who ever treated me with warmth and gentleness." A look of pleading flashes over her face. "But my mother spoke to me through Wanda. She reminded me of what I had done to her all those years back when I betrayed her. For once, I choose to be like my Mutti."

She laughs shakily and then continues. "I can hear her voice in my head right now, telling me that even if I kill Wanda, you will never belong to me." She raises her hand and presses the pistol to the side of her head. "She is calling at me now." She cocks it. "I beg both of you for forgiveness before I reunite with my Mutti."

My spine stiffens at her words. She acts as if she's in a different world already, her mind absent from reality. Is she on some kind of drug? I decide to speak to her in the same way she has spoken. "You have our forgiveness, Gerda," I say. "We all make mistakes, and I'm thankful for your mother's wisdom to bring you back from the dark side."

She stares into my eyes, but she still seems absent.

I'm determined to convince her to live. "I can assure you that she would want you to live. So she can watch you as the new Gerda, the one with an open heart. You owe your Mutti that much—to be alive, to do good in this world, as she did in her time."

Tears run down her cheeks. "How can you say this after everything I have done?"

"I believe in forgiveness, and I would have given everything for my brother to grasp at the same path to redemption you are trying to find, Gerda. Be assured that your mother forgave you all the way along because she loved you, and she knew that you loved her too."

"Drop your weapon and put your hands on the back of your head." Jimmy's gruff voice sounds like music to my ears.

His unexpected presence startles Gerda, but she doesn't drop the gun or press the trigger. There is something else reflected now in her face—an inner peace.

"Do as he says, Gerda. You deserve another chance," I say, flashing her an assuring smile. "We will not bring any charges against you. Please, believe me."

"I don't deserve another chance. If not for me, Mutti would still be alive. I betrayed her and everything she taught me." A sad smile curves her mouth. "And I forgot how to be a decent person."

Jimmy steps forward while Gerda stares at him. "Ma'am," he says in a calm, almost soothing voice, "just hand me over the gun, and I will take care of you. You will be in good hands. I promise."

She keeps staring at him.

"I know all of this is confusing right now, but after a good night's sleep, things will be more optimistic."

Optimistic? Come on, Jimmy. You can do better than that.

To my surprise, Gerda hands the gun to him. I have never seen Jimmy be so gentle with anyone before. He walks her to the nearest chair. "I apologize, but for now, I must tie your hands. Only until things get resolved." I like that he's so gentle with her.

While Jimmy is untying my hands, he says, "Ryan tried calling you so many times, but your line has been disconnected. We had a bad feeling about this, so he sent me to make sure you were okay."

"Good call. I'm so damn thrilled to see you."

He grins at me. "My pleasure. I'm glad you're okay."

With shaking legs, I spring to Wanda, gently remove the cloth from her mouth, and untie her with my trembling hands. I lift her into my arms, my heart drumming powerfully. "I'm so sorry, darling. I'm so sorry for putting you through this misery."

Our eyes meet. "You lost your brother." Her voice aches with sadness.

"A long time ago," I say. It's so comforting to hold her, knowing she is whole and safe.

She nods. "I thought we were going to die," she whispers in a weary voice, her lower lip still trembling.

"God has other plans for us, my love." I raise her chin with my thumb and plant a gentle kiss on her mouth. Her lips taste salty from all the tears she shed. At that very moment, I swear to kiss her in that exact way every day for the rest of my life.

Epilogue

Seven months later

Idlewild Airport, New York

MORE AND MORE PEOPLE BUMP INTO us, trying to pass by, but I'm unable to move forward. I just can't take my eyes off him, and this blissful warmth that envelops me deep inside doesn't help at all. His facial muscles tense as his worried gaze searches through the crowds of arriving passengers. He is looking for us.

When our eyes finally meet, an instant relief comes to his face, and my heart leaps. I hadn't realized how much I've missed him. It's been seven long months apart, but thanks to his determination, we're finally going to be together. I don't know what he did that put visas in our hands, but certainly it seems like a miracle that doesn't happen very often in the communist reality of my country. I just hope that one day Mama changes her mind and joins us. She has chosen to move in with Aunt Krysia and Uncle Mirek. I respect her decision but it breaks my heart to be so far away from her. I know it's not easy on Kubuś either.

Finn doesn't spring toward me. Instead, we gaze at each other in delight. I can't help but gasp at all the longing and admiration that emanates through his eyes. At this very moment, I dream of nothing more than his touch.

As if he can read my mind, he lurches toward and embraces me with such strength and gentleness it leaves me breathless. "You are here," he whispers and kisses me on the mouth.

I think I'm going to faint from the force of emotion racing through every nerve ending in my body. He deepens our kiss even more, leaving me drunk with happiness.

When he finally lifts his head, he grins and kneels in front of Kalina, who stands next to Kubuś and stares at us with confusion.

"Hello," he says. This is the second time I've ever seen tears in his eyes.

My little girl has a shy expression on her face, but she presses her doll to her chest and says, "You are my daddy, right?"

"Yes, princess." He picks her up and holds her tight in his arms for long moments. Then, he smiles at Kubuś and extends his hand toward him. "Hi, buddy. I've heard so much about you."

Kubuś nods and takes his hand. "Hi," he says and smiles at Finn. It seems as if they've already met, but I know they really haven't, besides the brief encounter the day I bumped into Finn after the roundup. It warms my heart to see them take an instant liking to one another.

Without another word, Finn pulls all three of us into his embrace, and I want this beautiful moment to go on forever.

· · ·

Thank you for reading *The Last Sketch*. If you enjoyed this book, I would be extremely grateful if you left a brief review.

If you would like to learn more about my next book entitled *The Faithful Tunnel*, please sign up for my newsletter at www. gosianealon.com.

Acknowledgments

Huge thanks to my amazing husband Jim for his support and for believing in me, and to my lovely children for inspiring me every day.

Special thanks to my wonderful sister Kasia and her beautiful family (especially my awesome nephews!) for always being there for me and encouraging me.

To my beloved parents, my brother Tomek, and my brother Mariusz with his lovely family, and my parents-in-law, for their continuing faith.

And to everyone else for their kind and supportive words.

My ongoing gratitude goes to Jennifer Caven, Jennie Rosenblum, Sara Kocek, Cate Hogan, Steven Moore, Lisa Orban, Shari Ryan, and my beta readers.

About the Author

Gosia Nealon lives on Long Island, New York, with her husband and two sons. She is an award-winner in the Genre Short Story category in the 89th Annual Writer's Digest Writing Competition. Her short stories have appeared in *(mac)ro(mic)*, *CafeLit*, *The Fiction Pool*, *Squawk Back*, and *Adelaide Literary Magazine*. This is her first novel.

Connect with Gosia
  Website: www.gosianealon.com
  Facebook: /GosiaNealonHistoricalFiction
  Twitter: @GosiaNealon

Made in United States
North Haven, CT
15 September 2022

24165639R00168